GW00750563

201227176

SPECIAL MESSAGE TO READERS

THE ULVERSCROFT FOUNDATION
(registered UK charity number 264873)
was established in 1972 to provide funds for
research, diagnosis and treatment of eye diseases.
Examples of major projects funded by
the Ulverscroft Foundation are:-

- The Children's Eye Unit at Moorfields Eye
  Hospital, London
- The Ulverscroft Children's Eye Unit at Great
  Ormond Street Hospital for Sick Children
- Funding research into eye diseases and
  treatment at the Department of Ophthalmology,
  University of Leicester
- The Ulverscroft Vision Research Group,
  Institute of Child Health
- Twin operating theatres at the Western
  Ophthalmic Hospital, London
- The Chair of Ophthalmology at the Royal
  Australian College of Ophthalmologists

You can help further the work of the Foundation
by making a donation or leaving a legacy.
Every contribution is gratefully received. If you
would like to help support the Foundation or
require further information, please contact:

THE ULVERSCROFT FOUNDATION
The Green, Bradgate Road, Anstey
Leicester LE7 7FU, England
Tel: (0116) 236 4325

website: www.foundation.ulverscroft.com

DEAD IN THE WATER

Although Jacqueline runs a successful acupuncture business in Windsor, her husband was killed in a car crash a year and a half ago and she misses him terribly. She could not have anticipated the drama that follows the arrival of her barge at the Black Swan Marina, or the growing attraction between her and Will — and she begins to dread the sight of the bird that appears after a killing . . .

Books by Irena Nieslony
in the Linford Romance Library:

DANGEROUS AFFAIR

IRENA NIESLONY

DEAD IN
THE WATER

Complete and Unabridged

LINFORD
Leicester

First published in Great Britain in 2013

First Linford Edition
published 2014

A catalogue record for this book is available
from the British Library.

ISBN 978–1–4448–2010–2

Published by
F. A. Thorpe (Publishing)
Anstey, Leicestershire

1

It was an unseasonably warm day for early May. Donald Forbes eagerly boarded the train at Waterloo station, relieved to be leaving the claustrophobic atmosphere of the city behind, but he was dismayed to find that the air conditioning in the carriage didn't work. He was slightly overweight, and because he perspired easily he didn't feel at all comfortable and soon felt his shirt sticking to his back. He wanted to get to his destination as quickly as possible, but unfortunately the train stopped at nearly every station. Donald tried to absorb himself in his newspaper, but it was futile. Then he tried to snooze, but it was too hot and the people opposite kept chatting. Young people were so inconsiderate these days, and he wondered if they really had bought first class tickets.

When Donald finally looked out of the window and saw the swans and ducks gliding by on the Thames and the parks and fields instead of the London buildings, he managed a smile. He was looking forward to spending the next few days with his brother, Arthur, and his sister-in-law, Penelope, on their boat, 'The Two Forbes'. It was moored at the Black Swan Marina in Windsor, and Donald was even more excited about the cruise his brother had suggested they take at the weekend. He hoped that Arthur would give him a chance to drive the boat as well. Arthur was very possessive about his craft, a very swish Sealine cruiser.

Arthur and Donald had been like two peas in a pod as young boys. Donald was the older of the brothers, but Arthur was the tougher one. In their late twenties they had started a business together. It had been very successful and now that they were in their mid-fifties, they were both very well off. A few years after they had launched their company, they had reluctantly invited their younger brother, Richard, to join them. Richard had called himself a free spirit, but really he was a bit of a layabout. Eventually they had become suspicious of him, believing he was embezzling money, and they had thrown him out of the business and had not seen him since.

Donald was relieved when the train finally arrived at Windsor station. Disembarking, he looked around for Arthur, but couldn't see him anywhere. Then he noticed somebody holding up a card with his name on it. He had absolutely no idea who this person was, but naturally he went over.

'Good afternoon, I'm Donald Forbes. And you are?'

'A friend of Arthur and Penelope's. Arthur unfortunately twisted his ankle this morning and as Penelope isn't coming down until tomorrow, he asked me to collect you.'

'Oh dear,' Donald said. 'I hope he'll be alright.'

'I'm sure Arthur will be fine. I don't think it's anything serious. It's only Wednesday today anyway. He said you weren't taking the boat out until the weekend and I'm certain he'll be capable of driving it by then.'

'I hope so, but I am more concerned about Arthur,' Donald replied, genuinely worried about his brother. 'Anyway, it's very kind of you to give me a lift.'

'It's my pleasure. Shall we go?'

* * *

While Donald was getting into the car of a stranger, Arthur was only a mile away standing by the side of the road, fuming. In fact twenty minutes before Donald was due to arrive at Windsor station, Arthur had disembarked from his boat, walked to the car park and had got into his six month old black Mercedes S600 V12. There was no sign of him having a twisted ankle whatsoever.

Arthur had smiled as he turned on the ignition of his precious Mercedes. He bought a new one every three years. They were his treat to himself for running such a successful business and they were well worth it. They were beautiful cars and so reliable. However, Arthur hadn't driven too far from the marina when he realised that the air conditioning had started to blow out warm air. He thought it a bit odd, but he didn't have time to worry about it. He didn't want to be late for Donald's train. Arthur didn't know much about the working of cars, but when he saw steam coming out of the bonnet he knew that something was seriously wrong. He stopped the car, got out, opened the bonnet and looked inside. Even Arthur could see that the engine fan wasn't working.

'Damn,' he said out loud. 'How on earth could this have happened? I've just had the car serviced. This doesn't happen to Mercedes cars, especially not to nearly new ones.'

Arthur paced up and down. He had been looking forward to his brother's visit and now what was he to do? He could ring for a taxi and go and meet Donald at the station, but this was a no waiting area and he could be booked. Despite being a wealthy man, Arthur hated paying fines. He was also concerned that his car could be vandalised if he just left it there.

'The youth of today have no respect for other peoples' property,' he mumbled as two young lads walked by laughing loudly and pushing each other.

One of the boys bumped against a scooter parked on the pavement and it fell over. He didn't bother picking it up.

'Hey you, don't just leave it there.' Arthur shouted.

'Why don't you pick it up then, granddad,' the boy shouted back and walked away.

'No respect for their elders,' Arthur mumbled.

However, he was shaking and knew he was getting too old for arguing with

6

youngsters. There was nothing for him to do but to ring his breakdown service. He got out his mobile and hoped they wouldn't take too long to arrive. Donald would be waiting at the station wondering where he was. Arthur shook his head, wondering why his brother didn't have a mobile phone. Donald had refused to buy one, saying he didn't want to be bothered by people calling him when he was out. He said everybody managed before mobile phones, so why couldn't they now? When Arthur mentioned the business and the need for a mobile, Donald said he was always in the office during the working day and people shouldn't ring him outside work hours. Anyway, they had Arthur's mobile number if they needed to call urgently. As much as Arthur loved Donald, he was frustrated by his attitude. Donald really did live in the dark ages.

Arthur was amazed to see the break-down service arrive quickly. Having told the man what was wrong, he sat in the back of his car hoping he wouldn't take too long to sort out the problem. He was surprised that his brother hadn't rung him from a payphone to ask where he was, but perhaps he had just called a cab and gone straight to the marina. It was the sort of thing Donald would do.

'Mr. Forbes,' the breakdown man said a little while later. 'It seems that someone has removed the fuse from your cooling fan and then sealed the fuse cover back down with super glue.'

'What?' Arthur exclaimed. 'Who on earth would have done that? And more importantly, why?'

'I have no idea, sir. Perhaps somebody wanted to stop you getting somewhere?'

Arthur was dumbfounded. All he was going to do was pick up his brother, so why would anyone want to stop him from doing that? He kept mulling it over, but couldn't think of any reason. It seemed crazy to him. Perhaps somebody had played a joke on him, not that it was particularly funny. The other boaters thought he and Penelope were snobs and that they looked down on them. It was all nonsense of course. It was just that they didn't have anything in common with the other people at the marina. Yes, that must have been it. Somebody had played a sick joke on him. He was going to complain to Daniel Harris, the owner of the marina, as soon as possible. This really wasn't on at all. He paid good money to stay there and what's more, he had offered to contribute to the construction of some new pontoons.

As it was still within the working day, the breakdown company took Arthur and his car to the local Mercedes garage. Luckily they were able to fix the problem easily. However, Arthur was still wondering why he had still not heard from his brother, so he tried Donald's home number to see if he was there. Getting no reply, Arthur convinced himself that Donald must be waiting for him on the boat. He'd visited there before so he knew where it was. It was a beautiful day and Donald would be sitting out on deck or perhaps he'd be in the bar having a drink. His brother was an intelligent man and would have guessed that Arthur would probably have had a problem with the car. They had only spoken on the phone the night before to confirm arrangements.

Arthur put his foot down as soon as he left the garage, but typically he hit rush hour traffic and it took him forever to get back to the marina. As it had been three hours since he had left, he was relieved when he finally parked up. He looked in the bar first, but there was no sign of Donald, and as Arthur walked back to the boat he started to get a slightly sick feeling. He couldn't see Donald out on deck, and when he reached the boat his fears were confirmed. Donald definitely wasn't there. He tried Donald's home number again, but there was no reply, so he then rang Penelope.

'It does sound strange,' she said. 'But

I'm sure Donald's fine.'

'I'm not,' Arthur replied. 'He was looking forward to coming to the boat. I'm sure that if he were going to cancel he would have phoned. This isn't like him at all.'

'I suppose you're right. Are you going to ring the police? Oh, you have to wait twenty-four hours, don't you?'

'That's just a myth, Penelope. You can report someone missing at any time. The police then decide how urgent it is. However, I won't ring just yet. I think I'll go up to Donald's house now to check that he hasn't fallen and broken a leg or something like that. If he's not there, I'll come back to the marina and phone the police.'

'Okay. I'll see you tomorrow.'

Arthur became even more anxious when he found that Donald wasn't at home. He returned to the marina and when there was still no sign of him, he phoned the police. They took all the details, but Arthur got the feeling that they weren't treating this as urgent.

After all, Donald was a grown man and not a missing child.

★ ★ ★

Two days later, in another part of the Black Swan marina, Kevin Wilson locked the door and got out a bottle of brandy and a small glass. He knew he shouldn't be drinking at work, but as he took a sip of the strong liquid, it sent a warm feeling coursing through his body and he smiled with pleasure. Anyway, it was nearly nine o'clock and his shop was closed. He really wanted to go home and couldn't understand why the books didn't add up.

Kevin ran the chandlery at the marina and he'd had a bad day. First of all, he'd had yet another argument with Jeff Carson. Jeff was the boss of the sailing boat franchise which was next to the chandlery and Kevin was annoyed that Jeff and his staff continually blocked in his car. There was no need for it, and Kevin was certain they were doing it just to be awkward. They didn't like him, he was certain of that. Today Jeff had accused him of scratching his precious Jag, but he hadn't. How dare Jeff blame him? Later in the day, Daniel Harris, the boss of the marina and of the chandlery, had stormed in and told him that his books were wrong. Daniel wanted them correct by the morning which meant his Friday night plans were completely messed up. He was looking forward to going to his local for a few pints and then playing darts, but instead he was stuck at work. Moreover, if that wasn't enough, retired police officer, Janet Price, had marched in just as he was about to shut, screaming that her gas bottle was leaking.

'You sold it to me,' she yelled. 'So you come and change it. I could have been killed.'

Kevin hated Janet. She was in her early fifties and was very loud. She wasn't at all well mannered and drank pints of beer, which no doubt accounted for her large size. To add insult to injury, she didn't even thank him for dragging another gas bottle to her boat and changing it for her. Kevin was fed up with both the marina and with the people there. None of them liked him and, to top it all, they all thought they were better than he was. He kept telling himself they weren't, but it still made him miserable that everyone had such a low opinion of him. Suddenly, a loud banging at the door interrupted his thoughts.

'We're closed,' Kevin shouted.

The knocking continued, so Kevin got up and went to the door. He recognised the person there immediately.

'Ah, it's you, have you got it?' Kevin asked.

'Of course I have,' the other person said. 'What do you think this is, a social call?'

'Be quick then,' Kevin snapped. 'We don't want anyone to see.'

However, instead of a wad of money being handed to him, Kevin saw a gun pointed at his chest. It had a silencer on it.

'What are you doing?' Kevin asked. 'Come on, this isn't funny.'

'It isn't supposed to be funny,' his visitor said calmly. 'Whatever would make you think that? You really have gone too far. Blackmailing both of us. No, I won't put up with it, I really won't.'

Kevin didn't have a chance to say anything else before he fell to the floor.

2

Jacqueline Lawrence stretched out in bed on Saturday morning. It was comfortable and she was relieved that she didn't have to get up yet even though it had gone nine. Jacqueline was an acupuncturist and she had her own business in Windsor which she had started six years previously. Despite a slow start, and Jacqueline almost giving up on her dream career, the business was now doing very well and she had built up a regular clientele. She had decided a couple of years ago that she didn't need to work at weekends.

Jacqueline was thirty-five years old and slim, with long dark hair and brown eyes. However, there was both sadness and loneliness to be found in those beautiful eyes of hers. Her husband, Jonathon, had been killed in a car crash a year and a half ago and she still missed him terribly, especially at weekends. It was the time they enjoyed the most, and lying in bed this morning she remembered the many weekends they had spent together on their Dutch barge. Jonathon would get up early and then 'surprise' her with freshly brewed coffee and pastries or croissants. She never knew which treats he would bring back from the bakery, but they were all delicious. Even now her eyes would mist over as she remembered those wonderful mornings. However, she knew she had to move on with her life and she had tried to make a new start a few weeks previously by moving their barge to The Black Swan Marina. Throughout their marriage it had been moored on the bank of the Thames, not too far from Windsor. Jacqueline and Jonathon had liked their privacy and hadn't wanted to be in a marina. They had their small group of friends and didn't particularly want to be part of a boating community. However, most of her and Jonathon's friends were couples and now they seemed to have little time for her. Jacqueline had been getting more and more lonely, and in the end she thought it might be a good idea to move to a marina, especially as she had also started to feel a little vulnerable living on her own on the river. When a mooring had become available at The Black Swan Marina, she had jumped at the chance. So far Jacqueline hadn't mixed much with the other boaters, but the previous weekend she had treated herself to breakfast at the café bar there. The café wasn't large, but in the evenings it was always packed with the regulars. Jacqueline thought that the couple running the café, Jim and Cassie Benson, seemed a very pleasant couple. They were in their mid-forties and he was tall and distinguished looking, with greying hair, while she was short, blonde and attractive. Cassie did the cooking, while Jim ran the bar. Jacqueline had noticed that they had pastries on the breakfast menu, but that brought back too many memories, so she had chosen a full-English instead. It had been delicious, particularly as it wasn't dripping with fat, and the thought of it prompted her to get out of bed. As she did so she looked at a photo of Jonathon. She had loved him so much and thought how unfair it was that he had died at such a young age, but she had been luckier than most people. She had had twelve special years with an amazing man and not many people could say the same.

Jacqueline showered and carefully did her make-up. Getting off her barge, she felt almost happy and had a renewed sense of hope. It was only May, but the sun was shining and the air felt warm. Last weekend had been cold and she'd had to put on a thick jumper and boots, but today she was able to wear a T-shirt and a skirt and had just draped a cardigan over her shoulders in case it cooled down later.

Approaching the café, Jacqueline saw a few people standing at the bar. At this time last Saturday, it had been empty.

She felt a little nervous, thinking that if they were regulars, they would probably all want to know who she was, but when she went in and sat down, nobody even turned to look at her. A few moments later Cassie came over looking agitated, but she smiled when she reached Jacqueline. Jacqueline liked Cassie. She had already found out that she used to be an actress and still did the odd bit of TV work. Cassie was outgoing, while her husband was more subdued and Jacqueline imagined that he was a calming influence on his wife.

'Hi there,' Cassie said. 'Lovely to see you again, but it's been some morning. I don't know if you've heard, but Kevin, the man who runs the chandlery, well I should say ran, was found dead this morning. Somebody had gone in and shot him. I believe the police think it happened sometime yesterday evening.'

Jacqueline gasped. She thought the marina would have been a safer place to live, but evidently it wasn't.

'I didn't really know him,' she said. 'I went into the chandlery once to buy something and he was having an argument with another customer. He didn't say anything to me at all. He seemed pretty miserable. Still, it's awful that he's dead, but who on earth would have wanted to kill him?'

'A lot of people,' a voice broke in.

Jacqueline looked round and saw a very handsome, tall and fair-haired man grinning at her.

'May I?' he asked, indicating a chair and sitting down before she had a chance to agree.

'Don't let Will bully you,' a woman said, moving away from the bar. 'He definitely has an eye for the ladies.'

'Now, Liz, you'll be frightening this poor soul away. I'm just being friendly.'

'We all know what your meaning of friendly is,' the woman continued.

However, she smiled and Jacqueline could tell they were just engaging in friendly banter.

'My name is Liz Boyle, by the way,'

she said, turning to Jacqueline 'My husband, Frank, and I come down to our boat most weekends. This scoundrel here is Will Phillips.'

Jacqueline was already taking a liking to Liz. She seemed natural and easy going. She and her husband, who was standing at the bar talking to Jim, looked to be in their late fifties, while she imagined Will to be around forty.

'My name's Jacqueline and I live on the Dutch barge that's just been moved here.'

Will and Liz both nodded as if they already knew about her, and Jacqueline thought they probably did. News got around boating communities very quickly.

'What did you mean about lots of people wanting to kill Kevin,' Jacqueline asked, looking at Will.

'Oh, I don't know about killing him, but he was always upsetting people and having arguments with them.'

'No, he wasn't the most liked person in the marina,' Cassie added. 'But to kill him, I can't think of anyone who would go that far.'

'Perhaps he had some deep, dark secret,' Jacqueline remarked.

'It wouldn't surprise me. He was a very secretive man,' Frank remarked, joining the group. 'Anyway, I think the police are going to want to question everyone who was at the marina last night, so I reckon anyone who was here had better stay put today. I think I'll need a big breakfast to set me up for that please, Cassie!'

'Right, Frank,' she replied.

'Why don't you all join me,' Jacqueline asked, feeling quite exhilarated for the first time in a long while. The circumstances weren't particularly pleasant, but it was an exciting situation and she felt alive again. However, she did wish that Will would stop looking at her. Granted, he was rather good looking and had a twinkle in his eye, but she wasn't ready for that sort of thing yet.

All four of them decided to have

cooked breakfasts and they moved to a bigger table. Once settled with their coffees and waiting for the breakfasts to arrive, Jacqueline started to ask more questions. She knew she was possibly being a touch gruesome, but the murder did intrigue her. She was also keen to find out more about Kevin. She had only met him the once and just remembered him as a very miserable man.

'So, tell me about Kevin,' Jacqueline asked. 'Why didn't anyone like him?'

'Well,' Liz replied. 'He was often rude to customers for no apparent reason and he seemed to hate his job, so why he did it, heaven knows. He seemed to snap at us whenever we went in the chandlery and I don't think I can ever remember him smiling.'

'Did he fall out with anyone in particular?' Jacqueline asked.

'Well, there was no love lost between him and Jeff. Jeff runs the boat franchise next door to the chandlery,' Liz replied. 'Jeff and his staff were always blocking in Kevin's car and playing pranks on him, and then Jeff found his Jag had been scratched. He accused Kevin, but it seems highly unlikely that Jeff would kill Kevin for that.'

'Then there was the business with the Forbes,' Will said. 'They're a wealthy couple who keep a boat here. A beautiful Sealine cruiser. It must have cost a bob or two I reckon. Kevin was overcharging them for certain things in the chandlery, probably for no other reason than that they're well off. I think he was jealous of them. However, when Kevin was in hospital for a couple of weeks, they discovered they'd been overcharged before and were furious. When he came back they threatened to tell Daniel, but I don't think they did in the end. I believe Kevin reimbursed them, but the Forbes have never been back to the chandlery again. If they need anything for the boat, they go to the chandlery at the marina up the road.'

'I can't really imagine anyone could have killed him for any of these reasons. There must have been something much bigger,' Jacqueline said.

'It wouldn't surprise me at all,' Will remarked. 'But I have no idea what it was. Nobody really knew anything about Kevin's life outside work. He wasn't friendly with anybody here. Ah, here are our breakfasts. Perhaps food will help our brains work better!'

They all tucked into their food, but were no further forward when they had finished. Seeing Will get up to get another coffee, Jacqueline decided to leave. He was a very disconcerting man and she was feeling confused. It was the first time she had felt like this since Jonathon had died and she wasn't sure of how to handle it.

'You're not going already, are you?' Will asked, as he came back with his coffee. 'Haven't you time for another hot drink?'

'I have lots of emails to answer, so I'd better get on with them,' Jacqueline said quickly, not wanting to extend the goodbyes. 'I've really enjoyed breakfast and talking to all of you. See you later.'

Jacqueline breathed a sigh of relief when Will sat back down with Liz and Frank. She had been slightly afraid that he might follow her. However, as she walked back to her boat, she couldn't stop thinking about him. What if Liz was right? Liz knew Will better than Jacqueline herself did, and if he was a bit of a ladies man, he wouldn't be the man for her. If she ever did get involved again, he would need to be like Jonathon. He had been romantic and devoted, but not boring of course. He had been fun and full of surprises. Will was fun too and he did have a nice smile. He seemed intelligent as well and she did like a man to have brains as well. Jacqueline was now feeling even more confused, and then the guilt set in. Was she betraying Jonathon?

3

John Stevens sat on the deck of his boat painting a picture of the bank opposite. There were a couple of oak trees over on that side and long grass with wild flowers growing in-between. A couple of ducks and moor hens had settled by the edge of the water, while a woman and her dog walked close by them, the dog, surprisingly, ignoring the birds.

John was lost in his own private world. He was a quiet man in his mid-forties, with dark hair and deep blue eyes. Although handsome, John rarely smiled and kept himself to himself, so most people didn't notice just how good-looking he was.

John was a professional artist and he loved his work, especially as he could do it in peace and solitude. It was such a lovely day, but instead of cheering him up, he felt miserable. He had been so sure that Kate Hunter was falling in love with him, but now he doubted his own instincts. As soon as she had met Daniel Harris, the suave and sophisticated owner of the Black Swan Marina, she had paid little attention to him.

Daniel wasn't better looking than John and they were about the same age, but it was amazing how much confidence and wealth could turn a woman's head. Kate liked a man to have power and money as well as good looks, but what she didn't realise was that Daniel wasn't a man who wanted to settle down, even though he was forty-six years old.

John had kept a boat at the marina for many years and had seen Daniel with a succession of beautiful women, so was almost certain he would tire of Kate. She would eventually come back to him and John was determined to wait for her, knowing she was still young and needed to experience life before she settled down. Still, he was hurt by her behaviour and it was distracting him from his work.

John closed his eyes and imagined Kate's beautiful face. Her hair was strawberry blonde and she had green eyes and little freckles just around her nose. He thought how cute they were. He remembered the first time she had walked into the café bar two months ago with her brother, Tony Hunter. She had put a spell on him right there and then. Kate was coming to the marina later with Tony and his wife, Lucy, and he was desperate to see her. Perhaps he could prove to her this weekend that he was more devoted to her than Daniel was.

Kate's brother, Tony, was the commodore of the marina's cruising club, but John didn't like him and thought he was rather stuck up. Both he and his wife were in their early forties, about ten years older than Kate, and were very thin and pale. Lucy was a very grim looking woman and he wondered what Tony could have seen in her. Still, Tony was no oil painting, so they seemed an excellent match. However, how could Tony possibly have such a beautiful sister as Kate? Perhaps she was adopted.

John went and got himself a coffee, and when he came back on deck, Jacqueline was walking towards his boat having had breakfast in the café. She was feeling confident for the first time in ages, having spent over an hour chatting to three complete strangers. She used to find it easy to talk to people, but since Jonathon had died, it had been hard for her to make new friends. At last a few people hadn't tip toed around her because she was a widow. She kept thinking about Will and how charming and attentive he had been to her, but then was he like this with all women? Liz had said he was a bit of a ladies man, but was he that bad? She would have to ask her more about him. Will had let it slip that he was divorced and had two teenage daughters and Jacqueline wondered how the marriage had ended. She hoped he hadn't had an affair. If he'd cheated once, would it mean he'd cheat again? But did it really matter if he had? After all she wasn't really that interested in him.

Jacqueline had seen John with his easel before breakfast and was curious to see what he was painting. She was very interested in the arts and she hoped the man on the boat wouldn't mind her looking. As she walked closer towards John's boat, she suddenly stopped, feeling a lump in her throat. From that distance, John looked so much like Jonathon, but she shook her head and as she walked closer to him, she realised that it was just his build and the colour and style of his hair. His face was completely different to her husband's. She knew she'd been staring at him, so decided to speak as quickly as possible.

'Good morning,' Jacqueline said. 'I hope you don't mind me coming over. I saw you painting and I was very interested.'

'Sorry?' John replied.

Despite Jacqueline staring at him, John had been oblivious to her presence. He had been completely engrossed in thinking about Kate, but suddenly he felt himself blush. John was a shy man and women didn't generally come up and talk to him. It certainly wasn't that he was unpleasant looking; he just didn't seem welcoming.

'Your work. I just wondered what you're painting,' Jacqueline asked.

'Oh,' John replied. 'I've only just started it, so there's not much to see.'

Jacqueline could tell that John was reluctant to show her his work, so she changed the subject. She never liked to pry, always believing that people were entitled to their privacy.

'It's a bit of a shock isn't it, what happened last night?'

'Sorry, I don't know what you're talking about.'

'What happened to Kevin from the chandlery? He was working late and somebody just went in and shot him.'

John almost dropped his coffee.

'I'm sorry,' Jacqueline said quickly. 'I didn't mean to upset you. I thought you would have heard. The police will want to interview everyone who was here last night. I don't think they have any idea who did it.'

Jacqueline paused. John looked quite pale and she thought he might faint.

'Are you alright? I'm sorry. I don't know your name. I'm Jacqueline Lawrence.'

'John. I'm John Stevens,' he whispered. 'Is Kevin dead?'

'I'm afraid so.'

John felt sick again. He hadn't particularly liked Kevin, but the thought of somebody being murdered in the marina frightened him. John wasn't a particularly brave man.

'Oh dear, I feel slightly sick,' John said. 'Kevin wasn't the nicest of people, but for somebody to kill him . . . He really must have upset someone badly.'

'Yes, he must. Everyone I've spoken to has said he wasn't well liked, but it was a bit extreme to kill him. Are you going to be all right, John? You don't look too good.'

'I'll be fine. I think I'll have a lie down. I'm sure I'll be better in no time at all.'

Jacqueline felt this was her cue to leave. As she walked to the next pontoon where her barge was moored, she tried to make out what sort of a man John was. Initially, it had given her a shock to see someone who reminded her so much of her husband, but he was really nothing like Jonathon. He had been self assured, funny and sociable. John was a shy and slightly frightened man who didn't seem to have much confidence with women. Jacqueline felt a little sorry for him. Life was obviously a hard slog for John Stevens.

John didn't go and lie down immediately. He watched Jacqueline walk away, and seeing her get on the barge, realised who she was and felt cross with himself. He really should have been nicer to her and offered her a coffee. After all, it must be difficult to be a widow, living alone and trying to start a new life. Still, he hadn't known who she was then.

Kevin then went through his mind. Now that was a surprise, but the man had it coming. He both upset and annoyed so many people and nobody actually liked him, but it was hard to believe that he had angered someone so much that they had been driven to kill him. John shivered, thinking again that there had been a murder right here in the marina. Was anywhere safe these days?

Jacqueline was about to get back on her barge when Sam and Pauline Dennison, her next-door neighbours, disembarked from their narrow boat. Jacqueline had met them on her first day at the marina and they had been very welcoming, making Jacqueline feel as if she had made the right decision moving her barge to the marina. The night before she had moved, she had been tearful, feeling as if she were closing a door on her marriage by leaving the place where she had lived with Jonathon, but she hadn't. Her memories of him were just as strong at the marina as they had been on the river.

The Dennisons had lived at the marina for all of the twenty years of their marriage. They were in their late forties and Pauline was a primary school teacher, while Sam worked in the city. She was short and a little overweight, while he was tall and lanky and Jacqueline thought they seemed very happy together.

'I presume you've heard,' Pauline asked Jacqueline excitedly. 'About Kevin?'

'Yes, I've been to the café for breakfast. Nobody seemed that surprised.'

'No, he wasn't well liked,' Sam, said, appearing behind his wife and towering above her.

Jacqueline wondered how he coped in their narrow boat, imagining him having to continually bend down. She would hate living on one, feeling they were too claustrophobic for her, but they were very popular both on the river and on the canals.

'We're just off for a bite to eat there ourselves,' Pauline said. 'Expect everyone's having a good old gossip.'

'Yes,' Jacqueline said, nodding. 'After all, I don't expect there's a murder here every day!'

Jacqueline smiled. This might not be the best of circumstances, but she was getting to know a few people and was starting to regain her self-confidence. She had to admit that she had been lonely on the barge out on the river. Initially, when Jonathon had died she hadn't wanted to get on with life and sometimes had wanted to give up, but she knew how much he would have hated it if she had shut herself off from the world. Although she would never forget Jonathon, Jacqueline did want to live and she was starting to get her energy for life back.

As she got back on board her barge,

the sun felt warm and Jacqueline decided to sit out on deck for a while before checking her emails. She loved the heat and had even toyed with moving abroad to a sunnier climate. Perhaps one day? She sat down and put her feet up, thinking how pleasant the day was turning out to be despite the news of the murder. After all, she hadn't really known Kevin. That morning she'd had a delicious breakfast, made some new friends and was now having a leisurely time in the sun. But what about the interview with the police? She wasn't looking forward to it at all. She didn't have an alibi for the previous night, but then why would anyone suspect her of killing Kevin?

Jacqueline tried to put all this to the back of her mind as she looked at the swans and ducks, deciding that the river and the marina were a stunning setting. John should be able to paint some amazing pictures. A black swan glided by and she thought how beautiful it was and how it stood out amongst the white swans. Then she noticed what looked like a big sack floating towards her boat and she became annoyed. Why did people have to throw rubbish into the river? However, as it got closer she stood up, realising it wasn't a bin bag after all and she started to feel sick. She wasn't completely certain, but she thought she knew what it was, and as it got nearer, she let out a loud scream. Not normally a woman to be easily shocked, she couldn't believe what she was seeing.

John, who had just lain down for his nap, but hadn't fallen asleep yet, heard the scream and jumped up. He had no idea who it was as he rushed out on deck and looked around. The only person he could see was Jacqueline on the deck of her boat. She was motionless, but her hands were covering her mouth. John knew it must have been her who screamed.

'What's happened? Are you okay?' he shouted over to her.

John felt ridiculous as soon as he

said this. Would she have screamed for no reason? He could see that her eyes were fixed on something large in the river, but he was unable to tell what it was. It had now got caught in the weeds on the other side of the bank and it wasn't moving. Jacqueline didn't answer him and kept staring at whatever it was, so he dashed below deck to grab a pair of shoes and then rushed over to see her. She continued to stare at the object in the water, but when she saw John, she moved towards him and finally spoke.

'It's a body,' was all she could say.

'Are you sure? It could just be a bin bag,' John said.

He hadn't even looked at it properly so why was he questioning her? Jacqueline wasn't an idiot and she wouldn't mistake a bin bag or anything else for a body.

'I'm sorry,' he mumbled. 'Of course you're certain.'

'At first I thought it was a bin bag full of rubbish as well, but then as it got closer, I realised what it really was,' she continued.

A few tears started to fall down her cheeks.

'There, there,' John said as he put his arms around her.

John's arms were strong and as Jacqueline looked at him, her heart missed a beat. What was wrong with her? She wasn't over her husband yet and now she was attracted to two men in one day. No, she told herself. This was just because John looked a little like Jonathon, that was all, and also he was suddenly being protective. He didn't have any of Jonathon's exuberance and confidence, and she hadn't felt anything for him earlier on apart from a grain of pity. She extracted herself from his arms and started to fiddle about in her handbag.

'I'll ring the office. I presume the police are still here as they wanted to interview everybody who was at the marina last night. Oh, John, I wonder if the two murders are connected. This is very strange, don't you think?'

John didn't reply. Despite trying to be protective towards Jacqueline, he really thought this was all very frightening, not strange. Two murders had been committed within days of each other and there could easily be a third. Then he thought about Kate, knowing this would be something that would excite her. Kate was a woman who lived for danger and if she knew that he had been around when this body had been discovered, she might be interested in him again. He would have to pretend to be brave. Perhaps this had worked out for the best after all.

Jacqueline put her phone down.

'The police are on their way over with Daniel. You'd better stay here, John.'

She looked away from the river and spoke again.

'Who's that couple walking along there?' she asked him.

Jacqueline pointed discreetly at a well-dressed pair in their mid fifties.

'That's Arthur and Penelope Forbes. They own that beautiful Sealine Cruiser three pontoons away from here. They're very wealthy and keep themselves to themselves. They don't often come into the bar, just occasionally on a Sunday afternoon. They think we're all a bit below them really.'

'Oh, I see,' Jacqueline replied, trying to see what the Forbes looked like, but not really being able to focus on them properly.

There really was quite a mixture of characters at the marina, she mused to herself. It was just like the range of boats, from the most expensive motor yachts to the tiny boats that barely slept two.

The barge then started to move a little and Jacqueline and John saw two police officers and Daniel Harris walking along the pontoon. John, seeing Daniel, felt rage bubbling up inside him again. He felt angry every time he saw Daniel. The meek and shy John turned into a completely different person inside whenever he was in the presence of the owner of the marina. So far he had held it in, but he was almost ready to explode. That man could have any woman he wanted, so why did he have to go after Kate? Daniel knew John was interested in her. In fact, everybody knew that John was in love with Kate. Of course, John wouldn't acknowledge the fact that it was Kate who was chasing Daniel. Daniel, if the truth were told, wasn't particularly interested in her. He still enjoyed playing the field despite being in his forties. Daniel was well off and enjoyed a carefree life and Kate was just a mild distraction when he was at the marina. He wasn't a particularly nice character when it came to women. He could see Kate was crazy about him, yet he just toyed with her affections.

'Good morning, my name's Detective Jameson,' one of the police officers said. 'You are Jacqueline Lawrence, yes?'

Jacqueline nodded.

'And this is?' he continued, looking at John.

'John Stevens,' John mumbled, still annoyed with Daniel.

'And the body?'

'Over there,' Jacqueline pointed.

The police officers and Daniel all went to the edge of the pontoon and looked towards the other side of the bank. The pontoons had been built in a row coming away from one side of the bank and there were boats on each side of each pontoon. An offshoot of the river flowed between the end of the pontoons and the other bank where the body was, and this offshoot lead to the Thames.

'No doubt about it,' Detective Jameson said. 'It's a body alright. Brian,' he said, turning to the other officer. 'Get onto the appropriate channels to have the body got out of the water. While I'm here, I'd like to question you two about your movements last night. Mrs. Lawrence?'

'I got home from work at around seven and I didn't leave the boat until nine thirty this morning.'

'Can anybody vouch for this?'

'No, I was on my own.'

'Mr. Stevens?'

'I arrived on my boat at five yesterday afternoon and didn't go anywhere until I heard Jacqueline, Mrs. Lawrence, scream a few minutes ago when she saw the body. I was on my own last night as well.'

Jacqueline grimaced. She didn't want anyone to know that she had screamed. It made her sound weak and she wasn't. She was starting to get annoyed with John and decided to have a word with him after the police left.

John noticed that Jacqueline's mood had changed and wondered if it was something he'd done or said. He was a sensitive man and didn't like upsetting people. It couldn't be because he'd said she'd screamed, could it? Kate would have screamed much louder and for a lot longer. She quite liked to play the helpless female, even though she wasn't, but perhaps Jacqueline didn't. After all, she had to look after herself and an enormous Dutch barge all on her own. He started to worry that he had been insensitive and knew he would have to make it up to her. Although he was in love with Kate, he didn't want to upset Jacqueline, knowing she'd been through enough. To apologise, perhaps he'd ask her out for a drink. She seemed pleasant enough to spend an evening with and if he took her to the café bar, Kate might see them and would be jealous.

After the police had gone to deal with the body, John stood there, trying to build up the courage to ask Jacqueline to accompany him to the bar that evening, but his lips wouldn't move. He didn't want to use her as that would make him a man in Daniel's ilk, but a drink in the bar would be harmless wouldn't it? She looked at him, wondering why he was still there. She was still slightly annoyed with him, but at last he spoke.

'I'm sorry if I upset you by saying you screamed. The girls I know seem to like being helpless. I can see you're not,' John said, hoping his apology would be accepted. 'Plus, I didn't even think of not telling the truth to the police.'

'That's alright,' Jacqueline replied.

John was right; he shouldn't have to lie to the police. She didn't know what she had been thinking. Also, she was surprised that John had been so intuitive to know why she had been upset. Perhaps he wasn't quite so different to Jonathon after all.

'Would you care to join me for a drink in the bar this evening?' John asked nervously. 'It might cheer us both up after such a traumatic morning.'

Jacqueline smiled, thinking it might be nice, but she also wondered why he was asking her out. She hadn't felt that he was in the least bit attracted to her in the way Will was. Apart from that one moment, she wasn't attracted to him either, but she wouldn't mind an evening out and it would be interesting to spend some time in the bar listening to the gossip about the murders.

'Why not, thank you.'

'I'll call for you at eight. See you then.'

As John left the pontoon, Sam and Pauline came back.

'We hear you've found another body,' Pauline said excitedly.

Jacqueline just pointed and they looked. Nobody said anything for a while.

'It must be connected to Kevin's death,' Pauline said.

'Yes,' Sam agreed. 'There's a lot more to this than meets the eye, you mark my words.'

'I think so too,' Pauline added.

'Perhaps you'd like a cup of tea?' Jacqueline asked. 'We can sit out on deck and watch what's going on opposite!'

Sam and Pauline accepted and were soon watching the police and forensics dealing with the dead body.

'I'm so glad we're over here and not there,' Pauline said. 'It really makes me feel creepy. How long do you think the body's been in the water?'

'A few days I imagine,' Sam said. 'A dead body sinks first as soon as the air in the lungs is replaced with water. Then it starts to rise when the bacteria in the gut and chest cavity produce enough gas to float to the surface.'

'I wish I'd never asked,' Pauline said, looking very pale.

'I just wonder who it is and if his death is connected to Kevin's,' Jacqueline added.

'It's probably just a coincidence,' Pauline said. 'That body could have floated a long way.'

'Oh look,' Sam said. There's Arthur and Penelope coming out on deck to have lunch.'

'You know them?' Jacqueline asked.

'I wouldn't say we're friends, they don't talk to us much, but they've been moored here for a while.

Jacqueline discreetly looked over and

wondered why they didn't socialise with the other boaters. She knew many wealthy people who didn't think they were a cut above everyone else.

A few minutes later, Jacqueline and her companions were disturbed by a commotion coming from 'The Two Forbes'. Turning, they saw Arthur calling out to the police on the other side of the bank.

'Stop, I'm coming over. This could concern me.'

'I would stay on your boat, sir,' Detective Jameson replied.

'Don't tell me what to do. I have to see for myself.'

Arthur jumped off his boat and dashed over to the other side of the bank in no time at all, surprising Jacqueline and her friends. Arthur was a large man who didn't look particularly fit. They then heard raised voices, but couldn't understand what was being said. Meanwhile, Penelope got off her boat, locked it and walked away. Soon she had joined her husband. A few minutes later, Arthur was allowed to look at the body and then he collapsed. Neither he nor Penelope returned to their boat that afternoon, but instead left with the police. Jacqueline, Sam and Pauline were left in suspense as to who the body was.

4

Jacqueline finished styling her hair while trying to make her mind up about John. Her first impression of him had been of an insecure, slightly frightened man, but he had been protective towards her when she had discovered the body, so perhaps there was a stronger personality trying to emerge. He also seemed to have similar intuitive qualities to her husband and she did find that appealing, but was it that important? They were just going out for a drink and she didn't have romantic feelings towards him, despite a missed heartbeat when he had put his arms around her. At that moment he had reminded her of Jonathon, nothing more, and she was certain that by inviting her out for a drink, he was trying to be nice to her after such an unpleasant experience. She didn't really think he was attracted to her.

Meanwhile, John wasn't thinking about Jacqueline at all. He was trying on a third shirt and he still wasn't happy with his appearance. He wanted to look sophisticated, but he knew he couldn't afford the same clothes as Daniel. Mind you, would Kate even be in the bar this evening? Daniel didn't often go there, or so John had heard. He himself hardly went in at all, that is until he'd met Kate. Come on, he thought to himself, he would be late collecting Jacqueline. Suddenly, he felt a pang of guilt. He was using Jacqueline and this wasn't the way he liked to act. What had happened to him since he'd met Kate? Jacqueline was a pleasant woman and he had to pay her some attention this evening whatever happened with Kate. After all, she'd had a difficult day.

Ten minutes later John climbed onto the barge and knocked at Jacqueline's door.

'It's only me,' he shouted.

'Come in, it's not locked,' she called back.

John admired the barge as he went on board. They had only sat outside that morning and he had been impressed enough with that, but the inside was even more spectacular. The boat was an early 20th century Dutch barge, which had been painstakingly restored.

'Your boat's magnificent,' he said loudly.

'Thank you,' Jacqueline replied from her bedroom. 'Both Jonathon and I loved it as soon as we saw it.'

The minutes ticked by and John started to get impatient. He was longing to see Kate. Finally, Jacqueline appeared and John gasped. She was completely different in looks to Kate, but Jacqueline too was beautiful. Her long brown hair had been curled and partly pulled back and her perfect figure was shown off in a tightly fitting black dress. For a moment, John was lost for words, but then he pulled himself together. What was wrong with him? He was in love with Kate.

'The barge was a bit of a mess when we bought it,' Jacqueline said, interrupting John's thoughts. 'My husband did most of the restoring inside, though we did have the outside worked on professionally.'

'It must have been hard work.'

'It was, but he loved it, and so did I, not that I was much good at it!'

Jacqueline smiled and her whole face lit up as she remembered working on the boat with her husband. John was confused. Jacqueline was gorgeous and he felt like taking her in his arms, but he reminded himself that she was thinking of Jonathon. She definitely wasn't over him so there would be no point in starting anything with her, but why would he want to? He still wanted Kate and he would only be doing it to make her jealous and to try and put her out of his mind. That wouldn't be fair to Jacqueline and John wasn't a bad person. He really needed to see Kate.

Then he would be himself again.

'Shall we go?' he asked, eager to get off the barge and away from what was becoming a difficult situation for him.

'Yes, I'll just get my bag.'

Within a few minutes they were in the bar. It was quite full, but John was pleased to see there was a table for two free. He didn't want to share pointless banter with other people.

'What would you like to drink?' he asked Jacqueline.

'Oh, a white wine please.'

She smiled, thinking that this felt a little like a date and now she surprisingly didn't mind at all. It was nothing serious, but she was enjoying being dressed up and being treated nicely.

Jacqueline looked around the bar and noticed that Frank and Liz were sitting with Sam and Pauline. Liz, noticing her, waved, and was about to get up when Frank pulled her back. He must have seen her come in with John and thought they were best left alone. Jacqueline felt strange. It had been a long time since she had been out with a man other than her husband. In fact she couldn't remember exactly when. Jonathon had been part of her life for so long that everybody else had melted into obscurity.

'There you are,' John said, returning with the drinks.

He noticed she seemed miles away and wondered if she was thinking about her husband. It must have been a difficult time for her, but before he could think any more about it, the door opened and Kate walked in with Daniel. At this moment, Jacqueline was looking at John and she saw his face fall. She realised there and then that he had feelings for this woman. She didn't know who she was, but she was very keen on the boss of the marina. Jacqueline was slightly disappointed by John's reaction to her. Although she hadn't really thought of having a relationship with John, she had been flattered that he had asked her out. However, she now realised that he was interested in someone else.

'Good evening everybody,' Daniel said loudly.

They all turned to look at him.

'Jim, make sure everybody has their next drink on me,' Daniel continued.

'Who does he think he is, Santa Claus?' John whispered under his breath.

Jacqueline tried to stifle a laugh, thinking that it didn't matter after all. She wasn't ready for romance and John didn't make her pulse race anyway. They'd probably be better off as friends.

'Shush,' she said quietly. 'He might hear you and you might miss out on that very generous drink of his.'

John couldn't help but smile. He had wanted to come out to see Kate, but he was actually enjoying himself with Jacqueline. She was an intelligent and humorous woman, and in different circumstances things could have been very different. However, he glanced at Kate, thinking how beautiful she looked this evening. Her long strawberry blonde hair fell over her shoulders in waves and her skin was lightly tanned, and oh, those little freckles around her nose. He remembered their first kiss. It had been a few weeks ago when he had walked her back to her brother's boat. Their lips had met gently and although it hadn't been passionate, she had stroked his cheek and promised to see him the following weekend. However, it had been a lie. All he had seen of her then had been a fleeting glimpse of her getting into Daniel's car. Was there really no hope for him?

'You know, you should fight for her if you're that keen, John,' Jacqueline remarked.

'Sorry?' John said, being brought back down to earth.

'If you really like that girl, you should do something about it.'

'Oh, no. Kate's nice, but there's plenty more fish in the sea,' John lied.

He didn't think it would be nice to talk about another woman while he was with Jacqueline. He was already feeling guilty about bringing her to the bar in order to make Kate jealous. However, Jacqueline knew he was lying.

Suddenly, the door flew open.

'So I hear that good for nothing Kevin Wilson has been murdered. Good job I'm here to sort things out. Pint Jim, I'll be with Sam and Pauline.'

'Who on earth is that?' Jacqueline whispered to John.

'That's Janet Price. She's a retired police officer. Used to be on the murder squad. Expect she thinks she can solve the murders herself!'

'She's a little overwhelming, isn't she?'

'That's an understatement!'

John became quiet and Jacqueline could see him watching Kate again. Unfortunately, despite John's obsession with her, she wondered if he and Kate were suited. Jacqueline studied Kate. She was wearing a very short skirt and a low cut top, and had a great deal of make-up on. She sat very close to

Daniel, occasionally running her hands through his hair. Kate seemed very exuberant and Jacqueline imagined she would need constant entertainment and excitement in her life. Would John be able to give this to her?

Jacqueline glanced at John, feeling a little sorry for him. He was intelligent and handsome and would make somebody an excellent husband, but he was quiet and a little dull. Daniel, on the other hand, was a gregarious man who liked to be the centre of attention. Pauline had told Jacqueline that he had married once as a young man, but it hadn't lasted long, and now he played the field, having no desire to settle down. Jacqueline also felt a little sympathy for Kate, thinking she might be expecting to have a serious relationship with Daniel, but that would probably never happen. Jacqueline then looked at John again. He was still staring at Kate, but he seemed angry now, and Jacqueline felt she should be too. After all, it seemed as if John's main purpose in asking her out was to make Kate jealous. However, it had been pointless. Kate hadn't even looked at him.

'Good evening everybody,' Will, said entering the bar.

'Come and join us,' Pauline shouted.

'Great, we'll have a good chat about the murders,' Will replied. 'Does anybody know who the body in the water is? I hear the Forbes rushed over to look at it.'

'Well, it'll be in the papers soon, so I might as well tell you,' Daniel remarked. 'It's Arthur's brother, Donald.'

Nearly everybody in the bar gasped.

'Good grief,' Will continued. 'I wonder if the murders are connected. I bet they are, though I can't imagine how. It would be interesting to try and work it out, wouldn't it?'

'I think we may have one or two amateur sleuths in here, don't you, John,' Jacqueline said.

'Yes, you're probably right.'

John now sounded a bit mournful

and Jacqueline was worried. His emotions seemed to be changing rapidly and he kept looking at Kate. Kate seemed to have completely forgotten about John, and Jacqueline thought he should try and put her out of his mind. However, she imagined he probably wouldn't be able to.

'Oh, hello,' Will said, noticing John and Jacqueline sitting together.

Jacqueline noticed that Will now looked a bit miserable and suspected that he really did like her. John noticed it too and wanted to tell Will that they weren't on a date. Why should two couples' romances be ruined in one night? However, Kate might hear and that would ruin his plans, but weren't his plans ruined already? John was confused. Surprisingly though, he had to admit that Jacqueline was an enjoyable companion, so perhaps he should pursue her instead of Kate. After all, she had agreed to go out with him and not Will. He didn't owe Will anything. In fact, he didn't even like him that much. He was much too chatty and popular and could get any girl. Why should he have Jacqueline?

Will, on the other hand, couldn't believe that the quiet and moody John had swooped in on the woman he liked. He headed towards the bar and ordered a double gin and tonic, thinking hard of what he could do to impress Jacqueline. He had thought they had been getting on well that morning, but now she was having a drink with John. What was wrong with the man? Had he just given up on Kate? He had been obsessed with her for ages and Will couldn't believe he'd just forgotten about her. Everybody knew Kate was only a brief fling for Daniel, everybody that is apart from Kate herself. He wouldn't settle down with her. Will knew that sounded a bit old fashioned, but although Daniel might be in the bar now, in reality he moved with the likes of Arthur and Penelope Forbes and Kate would never be accepted in those circles. Daniel was in fact a bit of a snob himself and would probably be ashamed to take Kate anywhere up market.

'Hey, Will, come and join us,' Sam shouted.

Will nodded. He knew the conversation would be about the murders so perhaps that would take his mind off Jacqueline. He wasn't even bothered that Janet had joined them. Usually he would try and avoid her as she was so loud and boorish, but she was an ex-police officer and had contacts. Perhaps she might get to know things sooner than anyone else did. As he approached the table, he noticed that Janet was on her mobile and was quite relieved that she was involved in something else and not dominating the conversation.

'Hello, everyone,' he said. 'Any more news about the murders?'

They all shook their heads.

'What's this then, Jacqueline and John on a date?' he asked, not really wanting to know if they were.

'A little jealous are you?' Sam asked, grinning.

Will found himself blushing.

'No,' he said all too quickly. 'I was just wondering what's going on. I thought he was crazy about Kate.'

'I don't know if it's a date,' Liz said defensively. 'John was the first person to help her when Jacqueline saw the body in the river, so I think they just got chatting. I don't think she's quite ready for dating yet.'

Liz had already become quite fond of Jacqueline and didn't want to see her get hurt.

'Her husband died a year and a half ago. I thought she'd be over him by now,' Will commented.

'They were very much in love,' Liz said sharply. 'You really can be insensitive sometimes, Will.'

Will became quiet. What a stupid thing to say. Of course there wasn't a time limit on getting over someone's death. He was relieved that Jacqueline hadn't heard him.

Personally Liz thought Will wasn't the man for Jacqueline. Of course, it wasn't up to her, but she was sure that Jacqueline deserved a more sensitive, loving man and she wasn't certain that Will was. He was always joking around and she had heard he was quite a ladies man. Although Liz liked him, she didn't quite trust him, but then she didn't know him that well. She wasn't sure about John either. They had been friends for a while, but he could be moody and unsociable.

'Well, that's interesting,' a loud voice interrupted everybody.

They all became quiet and turned to look at Janet. The room wasn't that big and her voice carried through as far as the kitchen where Cassie was preparing the food. Even she came out to listen to Janet's news.

'More info about Donald Forbes. He'd been shot as well. Arthur reported him missing on Wednesday. He was supposed to come to stay with Arthur on the boat for a few days, but he didn't turn up.'

Apart from some gasps, nobody said

anything for a few moments. Jim behind the bar was the first to speak.

'The murders can't have been connected then. Kevin and the Forbes barely knew each other, apart from them going into the chandlery.'

'I did hear Arthur and Kevin having a row about something, about being overcharged for various things, but it's hardly a motive for murder,' Will said.

'That wasn't unusual though, was it?' Pauline added. 'I know it's not nice to speak ill of the dead, but Kevin did short-change people and he was rude and always falling out with his customers. But I can't see how Kevin could have been connected to the Forbes in any other way.'

Jacqueline and John sat quietly listening to everyone. He suddenly turned to her.

'What's your opinion? Do you think it's completely unlikely that the murders are connected?'

'Not at all,' Jacqueline replied. 'There could be all sorts of links between them. It could be something illegal for all we know. Perhaps Kevin was handling stolen goods for the Forbes.'

John smiled. Jacqueline had a good imagination, but she could be right that there was a connection of some sort between them. He was having a much better time with her than he expected. Jacqueline was an interesting woman. He looked over at Kate and expected to still feel depressed, but he didn't and it surprised him. However, nothing substantial had really happened between him and Kate. They had just been to the bar a couple of times together and the romance had really happened in his head. He looked at Jacqueline and decided he wouldn't let his imagination run wild again. Perhaps he should direct his attentions towards Jacqueline, but he would take things slowly. He could tell she was still in love with her husband and wasn't sure about having a new man in her life.

'John, why don't you join us and

introduce me to your lady friend,' Janet called out.

'I knew it wouldn't last for ever,' John said under his breath.

Jacqueline grinned.

'Come on, it'll be interesting meeting her.'

John tried to smile as they got up

'This is Jacqueline from the Dutch barge.'

'Ah yes, heard all about you, pull up a pew. Believe you were the first to see the body in the river. Must have been a shock. Not used to it like me.'

'Yes, it was a bit distressing.'

'I think the force is pretty glad to have me on site to give them a hand with this. I'll have it solved in no time.'

Jacqueline could see both Liz and Pauline trying not to smile. She was glad that, despite two murders, she had moved to The Black Swan Marina. For the first time in a year and a half, she felt alive again.

5

Jacqueline woke up the following morning to the sound of loud voices. They were coming from the Princess motorboat on the pontoon to the left of hers, on the other side of Sam and Pauline's narrow boat, and luckily a couple of pontoons away from John. The boat belonged to Tony Hunter, the commodore of the cruising club. Tony and his wife, Lucy, had nodded to Jacqueline the previous weekend, but they hadn't spoken to her yet. She wasn't particularly bothered as there was something about them she didn't like. She couldn't put her finger on it, but she felt uncomfortable around them. She found it hard to believe that Kate was Tony's sister. Kate was very attractive, although in an obvious sort of a way, and very lively, while Tony seemed drab and dull.

'Really, Kate, you are an embarrassment,' Jacqueline heard him say. 'I have a reputation to uphold. Staying out all night with Daniel. It won't do, it won't do at all.'

'I'm thirty-two years old. I think I can do what I want,' Kate shouted back. 'And anyway, he owns the marina. It's not as if he's a nobody.'

'Hum, do you really think he's serious about you? He'll be looking for somebody sophisticated to settle down with, not an over made-up girl wearing short skirts and low cut blouses. Get inside now, we don't want everyone to hear our business.'

Jacqueline thought it was a little late for that, but she still hoped John hadn't heard. Poor John. He was hopelessly in love with Kate and she was glad he was. Going to bed the previous night, she had felt a little mixed up about Will and John. At some point or other, she had been attracted to both of them, but as she had closed her eyes, it was John's face that she had seen and she had remembered him putting his arms around her. However, this morning, she remembered Will's sad face in the bar last night when he had seen her with John and she recalled his cheerful banter over breakfast. He really did have more personality than John.

As Jacqueline lay in bed, it finally became quiet on the Princess cruiser. She wondered if she should go to the café bar for breakfast. She had spent so much time there yesterday that she didn't want to overdo it today, but perhaps there was more news about the murders and that was the place to hear it. She decided to think about it as she got dressed and put on her make-up.

Drinking her first coffee of the day, Jacqueline Googled the Forbes brothers. Donald's death had just reached the press, but there weren't many details apart from saying that he had been found floating in a marina on the Thames. The name of the marina hadn't been mentioned, which was a relief, but Jacqueline thought it would just be a matter of time before the press found out. Then she read about the clothing empire that the two men had created and there was mention of a third brother, Richard, who had proved to be the black sheep of the family. He had allegedly embezzled a considerable amount of money from the business and his brothers had thrown him out. Jacqueline wondered if the police had questioned the estranged brother, but where did that leave Kevin? Perhaps the two murders weren't connected after all. She decided to go and tell John what she'd found out, hoping he wouldn't mind being disturbed.

As Jacqueline disembarked from her boat, she looked towards 'The Two Forbes' and saw both Arthur and Penelope enjoying their breakfast out on deck. Their boat was three pontoons along from hers and she wondered what they had thought of the argument between Tony and his sister that morning. They must have heard it and couldn't have been impressed. Jacqueline was interested to see that Arthur hadn't been arrested for the murder of his brother and wondered if Janet had any more information. There were no sounds coming from the narrow boat next door, but Sam and Pauline had still been drinking in the bar with Janet when she and John had left the previous evening.

Jacqueline walked slowly along John's pontoon. She was a little nervous, not knowing if John would be happy to see her or not.

'Hello,' a voice shouted.

John was having coffee on deck. It was another surprisingly beautiful day in May.

'Hi,' Jacqueline replied. 'I hope you don't mind me disturbing you, but I've been looking up the Forbes family on the Internet.'

She went on to tell John what she had discovered.

'Perhaps this Richard guy has returned to pay back his brothers,' John said. 'It

77

could be Arthur next.'

'Yes, possibly,' she replied. 'But what about Kevin?'

'Who knows? He could still be connected to them in some way,' John said, pausing. 'I was just thinking about having breakfast in the bar. Do you fancy joining me? We can carry on our conversation there.'

'Okay, that would be lovely. I am quite hungry.'

Jacqueline wondered if there would be anyone else there who had more news about the murders. She was getting more and more interested in the case. However, when they walked in, there was just Jeff, the owner of the boat franchise next to the chandlery, sitting at the bar eating a bacon sandwich. He was chatting to Jim.

'Can't say I'm going to miss Kevin, but I didn't want him dead,' Jeff said.

Jacqueline thought everybody would probably try and cover their backs now, but then she'd heard that most people had fallen out with Kevin. However, it had only been over small incidents, certainly not things to kill for.

Jacqueline and John studied the menu and he then went up to do the ordering. When they got their coffees, Janet breezed in.

'Large coffee and a full English,' she shouted. 'Morning Jeff. Morning you two.'

Jacqueline thought how surprisingly well she looked. She had seen Janet down at least eight pints the night before and she was still going strong when they had left. Jacqueline imagined she must have a particularly robust constitution.

Janet plonked herself down at John and Jacqueline's table without asking. John was slightly annoyed. He had hoped to have Jacqueline to himself. He'd had a sleepless night thinking about both Kate and Jacqueline, not able to make up his mind about which woman to pursue. He was madly in love with Kate, but she kept hurting him by hanging around with Daniel.

Jacqueline, on the other hand, was beautiful and intelligent and was a much better prospect, but would she ever forget about her husband? And then there was Will. He liked Jacqueline too and would probably fight for her. Did he want all that hassle? John liked a quiet life. Jacqueline, meanwhile, wasn't thinking about John at all, but about the murders and didn't really mind Janet joining them. Despite her brusqueness, Janet was an interesting woman and she might have some information about Kevin and Donald.

'Heard any more about the murders,' Jacqueline asked.

'No, not yet. I have a good friend in the force here so I'm sure I'll hear something soon.'

The door then opened and Will came in with two teenage girls, no doubt his daughters. He just nodded towards Jacqueline and her companions, but inside felt both upset and angry that she was there again with John. Once he'd taken the girls back in the evening, he was going to go over and see Jacqueline and have a chat. He was a nice guy and fun to be with, while John was dull and boring. Everyone knew John was crazy about Kate, so Jacqueline was just second choice. What could she see in him anyway? John was so staid and boring. Will decided he'd have to prove to Jacqueline that he was much better for her than John.

The breakfasts came and while they were eating, a couple of police officers walked by. Half an hour later they walked back and a few minutes after, Sam and Pauline came into the bar.

'Did you see where the police went,' Janet asked loudly.

'Yes,' Pauline replied excitedly. 'They went onto the Forbes boat and took them downstairs, obviously for more questioning. Then the police came back up, but Arthur and Penelope didn't. We have no idea what it was all about. Haven't you heard anything else, Janet?'

'Not yet, but I'm sure I will soon.'

'I read that Arthur and Donald have an estranged younger brother, Richard. They threw him out of the company years ago,' Jacqueline said.

'Really?' Pauline gasped. 'Perhaps he killed Donald. This is so exciting.'

Janet didn't say a word and looked a little put out, indicating that she didn't know about this. Jacqueline felt a little guilty. She liked Janet, but the woman did like to know everything first, revelling in telling everybody what she had found out. However, Jacqueline was certain that Janet would now do her utmost to find out what was going on.

After breakfast, which ended up being brunch, Jacqueline returned to her barge to do some work for her business. Finishing, she decided to check the Internet again to see if there was any more information about the murders. The main news was about Donald Forbes, although it gave no indication who the suspects were. However, Kevin was finally mentioned. It stated he was murdered at the same marina as Donald, but it still didn't name the marina. However, Jacqueline was certain it wouldn't take long for the press to find out. Then Jacqueline gasped. Bullets from the same gun had killed both Donald and Kevin! She couldn't believe it. The murders were connected after all!

Jacqueline printed the page and dashed over to John's boat where she knocked loudly. He was dozing on the sofa and came to the door bleary eyed. John usually hated unexpected visitors and was scowling as he opened the door, but his face changed immediately when he saw Jacqueline. She looked so excited and he was certain that she'd spent most of the last year and a half totally miserable. How could he remain cross with her? Jacqueline however, noticed that he wasn't too happy and wished she hadn't come to see him.

'I'm sorry to disturb you. I just got a bit excited by something I read on the Internet.'

'It's fine,' he replied, trying to

reassure her. 'Come in. I'm always a little grumpy when I wake up. It just takes me a few minutes to come to.'

Jacqueline went on board and showed him the news about Donald and Kevin.

'Well, this is all very interesting,' John remarked, his face brightening up. 'But I wonder how Kevin is connected to Donald.'

'I don't know,' replied Jacqueline. 'Perhaps the estranged brother came back and threatened his brothers. He later killed Donald and Kevin saw him do it.'

'But doesn't that put Arthur's life in danger?'

'It could do, but don't you think the police have thought about that?'

'I would imagine so, but shouldn't they give him protection or something?' John asked. 'I haven't seen police officers guarding their boat.'

'Nor have I. Do you think we should go and talk to Arthur and Penelope?'

'No, I don't think so. They're not very friendly and never talk to any of us. They'd only think we're interfering.'

'I'd feel terrible though if Arthur were killed,' Jacqueline said.

'I'm sure the thought has crossed his mind already and he's talked to the police. They must have covered all possibilities,' John replied.

'I suppose you're right.'

She wasn't completely convinced, but it wasn't their place to interfere. The police dealt with situations like this all the time and they should know what to do. It was better left to them.

'Hey, if you're not doing anything, do you want to join me in some supper?' John said. 'It won't be anything special, but I'm not that bad a cook.'

John was a nervous man and couldn't believe he had actually invited Jacqueline to stay for dinner. He had forgotten all about Kate. At this moment in time Jacqueline was more interesting to him and he wanted to spend the evening with her.

'I'd love to,' she replied, much to John's delight.

While this was going on, Will was banging at Jacqueline's door. Where was she? She couldn't still be with John? What on earth could she see in him? All Will could think of was that he had to have a chance with her. She was beautiful and smart and John definitely wasn't the man for her.

6

'I think we should go abroad,' Penelope stuttered.

She was trembling and wondered how her husband could remain so calm.

'Don't be ridiculous, darling,' Arthur replied sternly. 'If he wanted to Richard would still find us, if it really was Richard who killed both Kevin and Donald. I certainly have my doubts. Why would he want to? He gets absolutely nothing from Donald or me if either of us dies. You're my sole beneficiary and your family is yours. And why would he wait so long to get his revenge on us for throwing him out of the business? He hated working there and anyway, Richard was always too lazy to pay anyone back. The police don't seem to think it's him; otherwise they would have given me protection. And as for leaving the country,

Detective Jameson has taken our passports, so we can't go anywhere.'

Penelope burst into tears, unable to believe what had happened in the last few days. Her life might have been boring before, but at least it had been safe. Now her husband was a suspect in two murders or even a possible target. But Arthur was right; Richard couldn't really be the killer. Then she smiled gently in amongst the tears. She could never forget Richard however much she tried. When she had first met him, he had been a smooth talking, tall, fair-haired and handsome young man. However, he did have a bit of a temper occasionally, but never with her. Although he was ten years younger than she was, she had loved him and she was certain that Arthur had never found out about their affair. Her life had become so dull since he had left and she wished that Arthur and Donald hadn't alienated him. No, there was no way Richard could kill anybody. He had hit Donald once, but

Donald had asked for it. No, Richard wasn't the killer. She refused to believe it.

Penelope looked at Arthur quietly reading his newspaper. He hadn't always been like this. No, when they had first met he had been very dashing and had taken her to the best restaurants, to the theatre and concerts, and had bought her beautiful clothes and jewellery. The first years had been good, but then he had got so engrossed in his work that he started to neglect her. When she had been unable to give him the children he had wanted, he soon tired of her and a series of mistresses had followed. He was discreet, but she knew about them, and that's when Richard came onto the scene. He had been the black sheep of the family and hadn't wanted to join Arthur and Donald in their business. Richard was a carefree man who didn't want to settle down, but when he was well and truly broke, his brothers offered him a place in their company.

For a while he had enjoyed it, but the wandering spirit soon took over and he started siphoning off money to save for his travels, a little bit at first, but then more and more. When they found out, Arthur and Donald threw him out, but by this time Penelope was head over heels in love with him and begged him to take her with him. However, he wouldn't.

'I do love you, darling, but you'll end up hating me. I get through money so quickly and always end up broke. You love the high life and would hate being poor. You know you would.'

'I'll put up with anything to be with you. I love you, Richard,' she said, her lips reaching hungrily for his.

Richard however, gently pulled away from her.

'Put up is the right expression, darling. You shouldn't have to put up with anything. Perhaps one day things will be different. One day I might make my own fortune and then I'll be back for you.'

She didn't believe Richard as she turned away, dejected. However, he was right. She did like the good things in life and wouldn't be able to cope with being poor for long.

Penelope wished these memories would go away. After all it was such a long time ago. She wiped away the tears and looked at Arthur who was oblivious to her crying. Sometimes she hated him and wished he were dead. Then she would be a rich woman in her own right and could find someone else to satisfy her in the way Arthur couldn't. She was so upset now and he wasn't even bothering to comfort her, not that she really wanted him touching her. Penelope had stopped loving Arthur years ago. When he had been diagnosed with the heart condition, arrhythmia, she was ashamed to admit she wasn't upset. Perhaps it would shorten his life and she could have a few years of freedom. She didn't even think of divorcing him. She was too used to a life of luxury and was certain that if she left him, Arthur would make sure she got as little as possible. He had the best lawyers and would punish her for deserting him, while at the same time he would deny all his indiscretions.

A loud banging at the door shook Penelope out of her own world.

'Who on earth is that?' she said, sounding scared. 'I hope it's not the police. I don't think I can cope with them again.'

Arthur got up slowly, annoyed that he was being disturbed. Couldn't he just read his newspaper in peace?

'Good evening,' Janet said abruptly. 'May I come in?'

Arthur groaned. What on earth did that woman want now? He didn't like Janet at all. It was uncouth for a woman to drink pints, and she was so loud and boorish. However, before Arthur could say anything to her, she pushed past him and went inside the boat.

'Hello, Penelope, how are you holding up? It must be a difficult time for you.'

Surprisingly, Janet and Penelope had developed an unusual friendship. A few months previously on a cold February afternoon, Janet had found Penelope sitting on a bench in the marina, crying her heart out.

'What on earth are you doing there?' Janet had said. 'You're not dressed for this weather. Come on, let's get you inside.'

Janet had marched Penelope onto her boat and they had sat there drinking coffee and brandies all afternoon. Penelope had confided in her, telling her about her failed marriage and how unhappy she was. Janet, despite her brusque exterior, felt a strange sympathy for Penelope. Janet wasn't one to put up with anything, but understood that others weren't as strong as her. She realised that Penelope was the type of woman who would find it hard to cope without a man in her life, however much she despised him.

As Janet stood in 'The Two Forbes', she remembered that conversation and felt like hitting Arthur over the head. He was making Penelope unhappy.

'This isn't a good time,' Arthur said gruffly, wanting Janet to leave.

'I've come to see your wife, not you,' Janet replied sharply. 'This must be awful for her. You're a suspect in two murders or you could be killed yourself. Haven't you given any thought to this?'

'Of course I have, you stupid woman. Don't you think I'm worried? My brother Richard might try and kill me.'

'A few minutes ago you were saying that Richard wasn't the killer, Arthur,' Penelope interrupted. 'Make your mind up. Neither of us can think of a reason why he would want to kill Donald. Don't you think he's waited too long to get revenge, and he's certainly not got anything else to gain, has he? He won't be left any money in Donald's will.'

Penelope had stopped crying and was suddenly annoyed that Arthur was being so inconsistent with his thoughts. What was he up to?

'No, but I've been giving it a bit of

thought,' Arthur replied. 'He could have killed Donald to put me off guard. I'm the real target. The business has nothing to do with it, nothing at all.'

Arthur spoke harshly, glaring at his wife, and for the first time, Penelope thought that her husband must have known about her affair with Richard. Janet looked from one to the other, the penny starting to drop. Did Penelope have an affair with Richard? Penelope was almost close to tears again and Janet thought it might be a good idea to get her away from her husband until he calmed down a bit.

'Penelope, I'm going to the bar for a drink, fancy coming with me?' she asked.

'Yes, yes, I would. And you can't stop me,' Penelope said, looking at her husband.

'I'd rather be on my own anyway,' he said, as they left the boat. 'Don't forget I'm going to the office later to get some work done in the peace and quiet.'

Neither woman bothered to listen to Arthur.

Walking up to the café bar, Janet spoke to Penelope.

'So, you and Richard?'

Janet never minced words, nor was she scared of asking personal questions. Anyway, it was too late for Penelope to deny anything.

'Yes, we had an affair. God, I loved him so much, but it finished twenty years ago. That's a hell of a long time ago. Yes, I think of him now and again, but he's like a dream, not a real person. And why would Arthur care now? Has he really carried all this hatred for both me and Richard for years and years?'

'Perhaps,' Janet replied. 'If he's kept all these feelings inside, they've probably festered away and got worse.'

'You know,' Penelope continued. 'I really didn't think he knew about us, but it looks like I was wrong. That must have been why Arthur sacked Richard and didn't want to speak to him again. It was nothing to do with Richard stealing money from the company. I always thought Arthur was going too far banning him from the family forever for stealing.'

Penelope had started crying again and she stopped to get out a tissue from her handbag to wipe away the tears.

'I really can't imagine Richard killing anyone though,' Penelope continued when she had composed herself. 'Yes, he had a bit of a temper now and again, but he was a good man and he wasn't spiteful. He certainly wouldn't have waited all these years to take revenge. Anyway, he was a free spirit and didn't want to settle down. He wouldn't have worked with his brothers for long. He loved to wander round the world. I wanted him to take me with him, but he wouldn't. He said I'd end up hating him. I loved the good things in life you see. I still do.'

'When did you last hear from him?'

'I haven't heard from him since he left twenty years ago. For all we know, he could be dead.'

Entering the bar, everyone turned, surprised to see Penelope with Janet. Frank and Liz called them over and they joined them. Penelope was nervous, not being used to mixing with the people in the marina.

'Hello,' Liz said, trying to make her feel comfortable. 'I'm Liz Boyle and this is my husband Frank. It's nice to meet you. Must be a difficult situation for you.'

'Yes,' Janet interrupted. 'Poor Penelope's caught right in the middle of it all. Worried for her husband, aren't you dear? The police don't know how to treat him, as a suspect, or as a potential victim. It's very stressful for you, isn't it? That's why I thought a few drinks would help. Take your mind off it all, if only for a few hours.'

'Such a good idea,' Liz added. 'You don't want to sit brooding about it.'

Penelope smiled. Liz seemed a very pleasant woman and she was sure that most of the other boat owners were the same. It was all Arthur's fault. He didn't want to mix with anyone. He thought they were all below him, so they just kept themselves to themselves. Her life was so boring. Arthur didn't want her to work and the only friends she had were the wives of Arthur's business colleagues who were affected and pretentious. She wanted to make friends of her own and then she would be much happier. Arthur had no right to tell her what to do all the time. It had to stop.

After a few gin and tonics, Penelope felt more cheerful, but she knew she should get back to the boat.

'I really should be going, much as I don't want to,' she said. 'I've had a lovely time, but Arthur will wonder what's going on.'

'Nonsense,' Janet said defiantly. 'He knows where you are if he wants you. Have another drink.'

'Alright, you've persuaded me,' Penelope said, smiling. 'I'm feeling much better already. I'll only be miserable if I go back to the boat.'

'I'm afraid I must go,' Liz said. 'I've got to go and see my cousin who's just out of hospital. Look after Frank for me!'

'We will,' Janet said, giving Frank a hug.

Frank gave a wry smile, disengaged himself from Janet and kissed his wife goodbye. Janet, Frank and Penelope stayed in the bar until well after midnight. Penelope returned to her boat and collapsed on the couch feeling quite tipsy. The bedroom was dark and she assumed that Arthur was fast asleep. Best to leave him like that Penelope thought as she drifted off.

7

Seven hours later, Penelope picked up her mobile and dialled 999.

'Good morning,' she said. 'Could you connect me to the police, please?'

She paused and waited for a few moments.

'Ah, hello. My husband is missing. I'm worried because his brother was murdered a few days ago and the same thing might have happened to him.'

Her voice was steady as if she were just ordering a takeaway. Penelope had woken up on the couch still fully dressed from the night before. It had only been seven o'clock when her eyes had opened, but she had a headache and desperately needed some aspirin. She wondered what Arthur would say when he saw her in yesterday's clothes, but did she care much anymore? Well, perhaps a little. Arthur had a way of

101

making her feel small and cheap, so she decided to creep into the bedroom and get some fresh clothes. However, when she opened the door, she saw that her husband wasn't there and the bed hadn't been slept in.

★ ★ ★

An hour later, Jacqueline got off her barge, heading for her acupuncture clinic. She saw Will coming towards her and didn't know whether to be pleased or irritated. He was a handsome man, but it had been a long time since she'd got so much attention from the opposite sex and she was finding it quite overwhelming. She sighed and wished she could escape, but there was nowhere to go. Jacqueline wasn't sure if she was ready for a relationship yet and had already decided that she wanted to ask Liz more about Will before she made any decisions about him. She wasn't keen on talking to him until she had, but she didn't have any choice now.

'Jacqueline, good morning,' Will said uneasily.

She was surprised to hear his voice tremble. The few times she had seen Will, he had been confident and she'd go as far as to say he was the life and soul of the party, but now he seemed a little shy. She found it quite appealing and thought that perhaps Liz was wrong about him. It looked as if it had taken him some courage to come and talk to her.

'Good morning, Will. I hope your daughters enjoyed their day with you,' she asked, smiling.

'As much as they can enjoy a day out with their old dad,' Will replied. 'I took them out on the boat and they seemed to have fun, but I expect they'd rather have been with their friends.'

Will relaxed a little when he talked about his family and a smile started to appear on his face. However, Jacqueline now started to tremble. Will really was gorgeous and she imagined him taking her in his arms and their lips meeting in a hot passionate kiss. However, she quickly pulled herself together.

'Was there anything you wanted?' she asked. 'I'm sorry to rush you, but I have to get to work.'

'Oh, yes,' Will said, becoming nervous again.

Jacqueline wondered why Will's mood had changed again and then thought he might be going to ask her out. She hadn't imagined that she would get this much attention from men when she moved to the marina, not that it wasn't flattering, but was she ready for it? She kept asking herself this question, but she knew deep down that the only way to find out was to go on a few dates.

While Will was trying to find the right words to ask Jacqueline out, she was trying to decide what to say if he did. Will was good looking and she was very nervous about spending time alone with him. However, he was fun, definitely more fun to be with than John, plus he seemed to have a vulnerable side. He didn't seem at all like the man Liz had painted him to be.

'Um, I've been given two tickets to the Noel Coward play in town for tomorrow night,' he continued. 'I wondered if you'd care to join me. It would be a pity to waste a ticket.'

Will looked so forlorn standing there and Jacqueline didn't feel as if she could refuse, though she did wonder if he was pretending to be so shy. Still, even if he was, at least he was making an effort and was asking her to go somewhere interesting, not just out for a drink.

'Oh, Noel Coward,' Jacqueline said. 'I do like his plays.'

'So you will come?' Will jumped in.

'Yes, that would be lovely,' Jacqueline heard herself saying.

'Okay. I'll drive, so I'll knock for you at about seven if that's alright?'

'Yes, I'll see you then,' she replied.

As she got in her car and drove to work, Jacqueline wondered if she had made the right decision. Will was obviously very keen on her, but she didn't want to rush into anything and hoped he wouldn't expect her to. Then she thought about John and hoped he wouldn't be upset, but then why should he be? He hadn't even attempted to kiss her the previous evening, so he must only think of her as a friend. He was in love with Kate, despite Kate's obvious preference for Daniel. If John were given the chance, he would be back with Kate in a flash and Jacqueline imagined that her image never left his mind, even when he had been with her. A relationship with John was out of the question and she had to admit she was quite relieved. He was a pleasant enough guy, but a little too dour for her. She had enjoyed her evening with him to a certain extent, but his conversation was very limited. John wasn't interested in politics, current affairs, sport or anything apart from the arts. She couldn't imagine that he and Kate would have much to talk about, but then talking with her would be the last thing on his mind!

★ ★ ★

Jacqueline's last client left at five, so she was back at the marina half an hour later. Approaching her boat, she saw Liz coming towards her.

'Not gone home yet?' Jacqueline asked.

'No, I thought I'd stay here and do a major clean up on the boat. By the way, have you heard the latest? Arthur's gone missing.'

'Good grief,' Jacqueline exclaimed. 'This is getting crazy. I presume the police have been back again?'

'Oh yes, they were here this morning.'

'This is absolutely unbelievable. Let's have a proper chat. Why don't you come on board for a coffee?'

'Love to.'

As the two women started to get on board, Jacqueline gasped.

'What is it?' Liz asked.

'It's John. He's sitting on his boat with Kate. What's more, they both look happy. It seems like they've made up.'

'Looks like it,' Liz remarked. 'And I thought you two were getting on so well. What a pity. It'll never work between him and Kate. She's much too flighty.'

'No, John will get hurt again, I'm afraid,' Jacqueline said. 'But he's not really the one for me, Liz. He's nice enough, but he lacks something. He's a little dull and boring. I'm sorry. I know he's a friend of yours.'

'Don't be sorry,' Liz replied. 'You've got to go where your heart tells you. Never settle for second best.'

However, Jacqueline was surprised that she was slightly annoyed to see John with Kate. On Saturday, she had felt as if John had used her to make Kate jealous, so perhaps he wasn't such a nice guy after all. She was beginning to think that she didn't even want to be friends with him.

Liz noticed that Jacqueline had become very quiet.

'Are you sure about that?' she asked.

'About what?' Jacqueline replied, trying to avoid answering.

'That you're not attracted to John?'

'Yes, definitely. Especially as he only turned to me when Kate was with Daniel. I don't think that's very nice, do you?'

'No, I suppose not. I would have expected more from John,' Liz agreed.

Liz was disappointed. She was hoping that John and Jacqueline would get together, but John was behaving very badly and Jacqueline deserved better. If Will buckled down and behaved himself, she would approve of him and Jacqueline. She'd keep an eye on him just to make sure.

'I can't understand what John sees in Kate,' Liz said with a hint of venom in her voice. 'She looks so cheap with all that make-up and short skirts. Tony is very embarrassed by her.'

Jacqueline was surprised by Liz's

outburst. She would never have put her down as a snob. However, she decided to ignore her remarks and turn the conversation to Will, knowing that Liz didn't really approve of him.

'I've agreed to go to the theatre with Will tomorrow, Liz. I know you said he's a bit of a ladies man, but he was very nervous when he asked me. He didn't seem at all confident, but don't worry, I'm not rushing into anything.'

'Don't get me wrong,' Liz replied. 'I like Will. He's great fun to be with. Just be careful. He is a bit of a player.'

'You've already told me that, Liz. I will be careful, but I am able to look after myself. We're only going to the theatre after all. Anyway, I'll put the kettle on, or shall we be naughty and have a glass of wine?'

'Oh, why not?'

As Jacqueline went to get the wine, somebody knocked at the door and Liz went to answer it. Surprisingly, it was Penelope.

'I hope you don't mind, Liz. I saw

you coming on board. I'm feeling terrible, not knowing what's happened to Arthur. Do you think Jacqueline would mind if I join you?'

'Of course not, have a glass of wine,' Jacqueline said, coming back in with a bottle. 'I take it you've not heard anything yet?'

'No,' Penelope replied. 'Arthur and I argued last night and I went to the bar with Janet. When I got back, I went to sleep on the couch so as not to wake Arthur. However, when I woke up this morning, he wasn't there. I thought he'd just gone off in a huff, but he wasn't on board this morning, so I rang the police. They've been to our house, but there was no sign of him. They've told me to stay here. I just can't believe Richard, Arthur's brother, is the killer. It sounds awful, but I thought Arthur was the murderer. With Donald gone, he would have the whole business to himself, not to mention the money. Donald had no wife or family and Arthur would inherit everything.'

'But what about Kevin?' Jacqueline asked.

'I just thought he might have seen something,' Penelope continued. 'That seemed the only likely conclusion.'

'But Arthur would be the most likely suspect,' Liz said.

'Yes, but he tried to blame Richard, which got people, particularly the police, thinking and now he's probably faked his disappearance. I'm scared he's going to come back and kill me.'

'Why would he do that?' Jacqueline asked. 'You're his wife and he has nothing to gain.'

'Revenge. I loved Richard you see.'

Jacqueline's eyes opened wide. She could never imagine Penelope having an affair. She wanted to ask more about it, but thought Penelope would think she was prying. Instead she continued asking about Arthur.

'So, what did the police have to say about all this?'

'They're looking for Richard now. They weren't sure if he was the killer before, but now that Arthur's gone missing, he's a more likely suspect. They asked for a photo of him, but the last one I have is twenty years old and he must have changed a lot. I probably wouldn't recognise him if he walked in now. Oh God, I suppose they think that he could have killed Arthur and then planned to marry me. Then he would be really rich. As if I'd fall for that. How could he imagine I'd still be in love with him after all these years? As I said, I wouldn't even recognise him.'

Jacqueline was completely engrossed. There were so many possibilities. Perhaps Richard came back and killed Donald and then killed Arthur in revenge for being thrown out of the business. But why had he left it so long? Did he plan to woo Penelope and marry her, therefore becoming a very wealthy man? Perhaps Kevin saw him kill Donald so he had to die also. However, Arthur could have murdered Donald for the money and framed Richard. Perhaps Arthur faked his disappearance to direct the blame onto the missing brother.

Penelope had started crying and Liz went over to comfort her.

'Do you want to stay on my boat tonight, dear?' she asked. 'You might feel safer?'

'Thank you, but the police told me to stay put, so I'd better stay on my own boat. Thank you. I'll be fine, I'm sure I will.'

'Well stay and have some dinner here, both of you,' Jacqueline said. 'I have plenty of wine. We can have a girls evening in.'

Both women agreed and Jacqueline felt relieved that she wasn't going to have an evening alone thinking about Will and John. She knew she could ponder too much and she didn't want to. She had imagined that she had put all thoughts of romance behind her years ago.

By the time eleven o'clock came, Penelope was falling asleep after indulging in too many glasses of wine.

Drinking too much two nights in a row, Penelope thought. Arthur would have a fit. She giggled, even though she knew she should be serious. Arthur was missing after all.

'Come on, Penelope,' Liz said. 'I'll help you to your boat.'

'Oh dear,' Penelope replied sleepily. 'I'm making a habit of this. I've had too much to drink again.'

'Don't worry about it,' Jacqueline said. 'You've been through a lot these past few days.'

'It's not been the best of times, no. Well, thank you so much for dinner,' Penelope replied, trying to keep awake.

Liz and Penelope got off the barge, while Jacqueline went on deck to make sure they managed to walk along the pontoon safely. All of a sudden, Penelope woke up completely and shouted out.

'Arthur, it's Arthur. Where've you been, Arthur?'

'Shut up, you stupid woman, you'll be waking everybody up,' he replied.

'Don't talk to your wife like that,' Liz said sharply. 'We've all been worried. She called the police this morning, thinking you were dead.'

'The police, my God, whatever for. Are you mad?'

Penelope started to cry. Jacqueline ran down the pontoon, and put her arm around her.

'You weren't on the boat this morning,' Jacqueline said. 'Penelope thought you had been murdered.'

'I told you I had to go into work last night.'

'I didn't remember,' Penelope answered. 'But why didn't you come back afterwards?'

'It was after three when I finished, so I slept there as I had to go up north on business this morning. You knew that.'

'I forgot. I rang you at home and on your mobile. You didn't answer.'

'The battery ran out on my mobile and I'd left my charger here. We'd better ring the police. They're really going to think we're barmy.'

116

'Better to be safe than sorry,' Liz put in.

Arthur glared at her.

'Come on Penelope, let's get this over and done with.'

Liz and Jacqueline watched them go.

'I don't envy Penelope tonight,' Jacqueline said.

'Nor do I,' Liz added. 'It would probably have been better if Arthur had never come back.'

Jacqueline looked at her expressionless face, surprised to hear Liz say something so nasty.

8

It was almost seven on Tuesday evening
and Jacqueline wasn't ready for her
evening out with Will. She had tried on
lots of outfits and none of them looked
right. She either felt overdressed or
underdressed or she thought she looked
fat even though she was a very slim
woman. Will would be here in a few
minutes and she didn't want to have to
ask him to wait. They could be late for
the theatre and wouldn't be let in until
the interval which would be very
disappointing and a complete waste of
time. Will wouldn't be pleased with her
and would probably never ask her out
again. However, Jacqueline didn't know
why she was making such a fuss over
her appearance. She told herself she
didn't particularly want to impress Will.
He had to take her as he found her.

'There,' she said out loud at last.

'That looks fine.'

Jacqueline was wearing a red skirt that came just above her knees. She had good legs and there was no point in hiding them. She had put on a cream silk blouse that showed off a light tan and she decided to take a short red jacket in case it got cool later on. It was still warm for the time of year, but in May the nights usually got cool. She then grabbed her red handbag and red high-heeled shoes. Jacqueline had become very adept at walking along the pontoons in heels, although she thought that when winter came with the possibility of ice and snow, she would put on sensible shoes to walk along the pontoons and carry her heeled shoes in a bag to change into later. She hadn't had this problem living on the bank of the Thames where she had got off straight onto a path.

There was a knock at the door and Jacqueline suddenly felt nervous. However, when she opened the door, she looked cool, calm and certainly not flustered. She seemed poised and self-assured as if she had been ready for hours!

'Good evening,' Will said, trying not to stare. 'These are for you.'

He held out a beautiful bunch of red roses and Jacqueline was more than impressed. Whether or not this was a proper date, Will was being a total gentleman and she certainly didn't mind. He was wearing a navy suit, with a white shirt and a pale blue tie. This was the first time Jacqueline had seen Will in a suit and she trembled. He looked absolutely gorgeous, even more handsome than in his casual clothes. She started to imagine his lips reaching for hers and his arms closing around her, his hands starting to stroke her back and then his lips kissing her neck, but then she forced herself back to the present.

'They're beautiful,' she exclaimed, taking the roses. 'I'll put them in water and then we'd better go. We don't want to be late, do we?'

Will shook his head. For once, he was tongue-tied.

★ ★ ★

The evening went better than Jacqueline could have hoped. There was time to have a drink before the show and they had excellent seats in the theatre. They both thoroughly enjoyed the play and when Will offered to take Jacqueline for a cocktail afterwards, she accepted. He was courteous and polite and she was amazed at what a wonderful time she was having and also that she didn't feel guilty. Jacqueline felt that Jonathon would approve. Despite his nervousness at asking her out, Will was generally confident and he certainly knew how to treat Jacqueline and make her feel special. She thought briefly about John and realised that she had only felt a pull towards him because he had looked a little like her husband. However, he was too shy and dull for her and he had used her. Perhaps it was better that she avoided his company in the future.

'So, that was a strange business with Arthur.' Will said as they sat down with their cocktails.

'It really was,' Jacqueline replied.

'I would have thought he would have phoned Penelope from somewhere to let her know he was alright, don't you? I know his mobile wasn't working, but it's not that difficult to find a phone,' Will said. 'Under the circumstances, it's not surprising that Penelope was worried and called the police.'

'I think their marriage is on pretty shaky ground,' Jacqueline remarked. 'So perhaps he was trying to teach her a lesson. He did say he told her he was going to work, but she said she didn't hear him. However, I also would have thought he would have phoned her the following day. Perhaps he's done something like that before, but Penelope got worried this time because Donald had been murdered. It's not surprising really.'

Jacqueline paused, trying to decide whether to confide in him another piece of information. Finally, she spoke.

'Can I tell you something in confidence?'

'Of course. You can trust me, Jacqueline.'

Somehow, although she didn't know him that well, Jacqueline felt she could rely on Will.

'Arthur and Donald had a younger brother, Richard, who worked for them. However, he stole money from the business and was sacked. He left the country and was never seen again, but that wasn't all. He also had an affair with Penelope.'

Will's eyes opened wide.

'It wouldn't surprise me if Richard is back on the scene and killed Donald and intends to kill Arthur,' Jacqueline continued. 'I don't know what he hopes to gain. Penelope inherits everything if Arthur dies.'

'Perhaps Richard intends to woo Penelope back.'

'But wouldn't that make him a prime suspect in the murders?'

'I suppose it would, but if the police can't find any proof, there'll be nothing they can do.'

'True,' Jacqueline remarked. 'And who's to say Penelope would take him back. She seems a very intelligent woman. Of course, she could have known all about it and she could have organised it with Richard. She said she hadn't seen him for twenty years, but she could be lying.'

'That's a bit far-fetched,' Will said.

'But you never know. They could have kept in touch, or he could have contacted her recently and opened up a can of worms. There's a whole range of possibilities.'

Will wondered why Jacqueline was so interested in finding out who the murderer was, but he found it quite sweet, although he would never tell her that. Women hated being thought of as sweet. Instead, he carried on talking about Penelope.

'You said earlier you saw Penelope last night?'

'Yes, she was very upset. I invited her for dinner on the barge. Liz Boyle was there as well. Penelope did cheer up after a few glasses of wine, but when they both got off the boat to go to bed, they saw Arthur walking back to his boat.'

'It all seems very complicated to me, Jacqueline,' Will said. 'It's probably better left to the police, don't you think?'

'Yes, you're probably right,' Jacqueline replied, a bit disappointed that Will wasn't that interested in talking about the murders. 'Oh, I know what I was going to ask you. I heard the sail past was supposed to be this Sunday. Is it still going ahead?'

'Oh yes. Tony won't let anything stop it. Thinks it will bind the boating community together after the tragedies that have befallen us. That was how he put it anyway. I wouldn't exactly call them tragedies though, would you? Yes, it's sad that two people have died, but nobody except for the Forbes knew Donald and nobody liked Kevin . . . Will you be going to the sail past, Jacqueline?'

'Well, I'll be going to the bar after, but I won't take my boat on the river. It really is too big to navigate on my own.'

Jacqueline's barge was 80ft long and needed more than one person to crew.

'Why don't you join me on my boat?' Will asked, hoping excitedly that she'd say yes. 'I tried to get my girls to come, but they made excuses. Jeff from the sailing franchise is coming with me as well, but it would be nice if you could join us.'

Jacqueline had never been on a sail past and had wanted to go, so didn't hesitate to give Will an answer.

'Thank you; that would be lovely.'

Of course, she had also enjoyed her evening with Will and did want to spend more time with him, so this was an ideal opportunity. The evening had been wonderful and she wished people wouldn't interfere. Liz had given her opinion of Will and although Jacqueline always made up her own mind about others, what people said still did lurk in the corners of her mind. This evening had proved it was worth giving people a chance as they could surprise you.

★   ★   ★

As Will walked Jacqueline down her pontoon, she felt nervous and didn't know what to do. She certainly didn't want the relationship to progress any further than a goodnight kiss, but it had been so long since she had been on a date, that she didn't know if she should still invite him in for a coffee. Luckily, Will was aware of her predicament.

'I've really enjoyed this evening, thank you Jacqueline, but I won't come in. I've got to be up very early to go to Birmingham on business. I'll be back at the weekend for the sail past.'

'I'm looking forward to it,' Jacqueline said, smiling.

Will looked at her. She seemed a little lost and vulnerable and he knew that this was difficult for her. He didn't want to frighten her away so he stroked her cheek and then brushed his lips gently against hers, feeling that this was enough for the time being. Jacqueline felt herself shiver. This was romantic, but then, for the first time this evening, she felt a pang of guilt. She knew she shouldn't as Jonathon had been dead for a year and a half and he would want her to move on, but she felt as if she were betraying him. This would take time and she hoped Will would be patient with her.

'Well,' he said. 'I'll see you soon then.'

'Yes,' Jacqueline replied. 'Have a good week.'

She didn't know what else to say. She got on board her barge and stood watching Will walking back along the pontoon.

* * *

John had been inside his boat all evening. He had thought everything was back on track with Kate after she had had another row with Daniel. She had been expecting to be his date for the sail past, but he was taking the local Member of Parliament. Kate was very jealous and had fought with Daniel. Granted the M.P. was older than Daniel, but only by a couple of years and she looked good for her age. She was sophisticated and divorced and while Daniel denied being attracted to her, Kate thought differently and ran to John for comfort. She knew John was crazy about her, well that was before he had met Jacqueline. Still, John had only turned to Jacqueline on the rebound. Kate knew she would be able to get John back and she had. They had spent a wonderful night together, but then Daniel had sent her roses and chocolates and promised that the weekend after the sail past, they would go to Paris together. He had even showed her the tickets. How would she tell John?

They were supposed to be going out to dinner on Tuesday evening, but she had phoned to tell him she was sick and instead spent the evening with Daniel. John tried to pin her down for another evening, but she said she didn't know when she'd be feeling better. She wouldn't even commit to the sail past and thought she might as well go with her brother. Kate was starting to make excuses again and John was getting worried. She'd done this before when she had started seeing Daniel behind his back. Was this happening again?

While John sat there thinking, he looked out of the window and saw Will and Jacqueline walking back together to her boat. He frowned. He didn't like Will. What on earth could Jacqueline see in him? He was cocky and thought too much of himself. Will thought he could get any woman he wanted. John carried on watching and was relieved when he saw Jacqueline get on her boat alone. He didn't think she was ready for anything serious yet, and from talking to her it was obvious she still had strong feelings for her dead husband. He did like her and in different circumstances they could have been good together. That is, if she didn't still love her husband and if he wasn't obsessed with Kate . . . ..

9

On Saturday evening Arthur told Penelope he was going to the marina with her on the Sunday. He hadn't planned to, but he had changed his mind. However, he had no intention of taking his boat out on the river to take part in the sail past. Instead, he had made arrangements to see Daniel. Also, Penelope wanted to see her new and very unsuitable friends and he wanted to keep an eye on her.

Arthur and Penelope had returned to their home in West London on Wednesday morning and the rest of the week had gone by rather quietly. There had been no developments in the murder enquiries and no attempts on their lives. It was as if the previous week hadn't happened.

On Sunday morning, Penelope emerged from the bedroom. She

looked pale and drawn.

'Arthur, I really don't think I'll be able to go to the boat today. I've got the most awful headache. In fact, I'm sure it's a migraine. I think it's better I stay in bed today with the curtains closed. I'm so disappointed,' she said, almost in tears. 'I was looking forward to going to the boat. I'm starting to get on so well with the girls, especially Janet and Jacqueline. Jacqueline's been through such an awful time, what with losing her husband at such a young age. It's been terrible for her, but she's such a brave young woman. She's picked herself up and started a new life on her own. I don't think I could cope as well as she has.'

'I really don't know why you want to be friends with those women, Penelope. Jacqueline seems fine, but the rest of them . . . But it's your choice, not mine. Anyway, if you don't mind, I'll go down to the boat on my own a bit later on.'

'You will? I didn't think you were

interested in the sail past?'

'I'm not particularly, but Daniel phoned to say he has some people coming to the marina today who may be interested in placing orders with our company. I would like to see if anything comes of this or if Daniel's just all talk. I'm not sure about that man.'

Penelope went back into the bedroom, a smile appearing on her face. She had overheard his conversation with Daniel a couple of days previously when she had picked up the extension. She hadn't known Arthur was on the phone, but what a stroke of luck to have caught him arranging to meet Daniel on Sunday.

★　★　★

Around one o'clock, Arthur left Penelope asleep in their darkened bedroom. As long as there wasn't too much traffic, it was about three quarter's of an hour's drive to Windsor. About half an hour after her husband had left;

Penelope got up and picked up the phone.

'Richard, Arthur's gone for the afternoon. Can you come over? I'm so looking forward to seeing you at last.'

The doorbell rang fifteen minutes later, and Penelope, shaking, went to answer it. A tall, slim man stood there and despite not having seen him for twenty years, Penelope thought he had hardly changed. There were a few more lines on his face, but they gave him a rugged appearance, and the streaks of grey in his dark brown hair made him look distinguished. Richard still saw the pretty, fair-haired woman of twenty years ago and the fact that she had put on a few pounds didn't bother him. A little surgery had taken care of the inevitable aging of even the most beautiful face.

Richard and Penelope stood staring at each other for a few moments, but it seemed like an eternity. Finally, they melted into each other's arms as if they had never been apart.

'I can't believe I'm holding you again after so many years,' Richard said, running his hands through her hair.

'When you left twenty years ago, I thought we'd never see each other again,' Penelope replied. 'Come inside, before anyone sees you.'

Richard went in and they sat together on the sofa, holding hands without speaking for a few moments. Eventually, Richard started to talk quietly.

'I wanted to get in touch with you so many times this past year, ever since I came back to England, but I didn't want to stir up trouble between you and Arthur. When I heard about Donald's murder, I had to call you. I was so afraid Arthur would answer the phone, but when I heard your voice, I was so relieved.'

'I was afraid you had killed Donald.'

'Why would I have killed him, Penelope? What for? Do you think I would wait twenty years to get revenge? Unfortunately however, I haven't got an alibi for his murder, but believe me, I didn't kill him. You do know that I'm telling the truth, don't you?'

Penelope looked at Richard and she did believe him. Gazing into those eyes of his, she would believe anything he said. Penelope realised that she still loved Richard after all these years.

'If I was going to kill anyone, it would be Arthur,' he continued.

'That would be crazy,' Penelope exclaimed. 'I can divorce Arthur. I want you to be with me, not in prison!'

'I didn't mean it. Calm down, darling. I don't intend to kill anyone. And then there's Kevin, why on earth would I kill him? I can't think how he's connected to Donald or Arthur or this whole situation, can you? But I read that the bullets came from the same gun. Perhaps Kevin saw who killed Donald and he had to be silenced.'

Penelope nodded.

'It's the only explanation,' she said. 'However, I think the police think I could be the murderer, though they haven't got any proof.'

'What?' Richard exclaimed.

'I haven't got an alibi for Donald's murder. I was here alone in London. Arthur and I were together while Kevin was being killed, so Arthur is my alibi, but that doesn't count for much. The police have asked me so many questions, but they didn't arrest me. I'm sure that I'm the prime suspect at the moment, but I didn't kill anyone. Richard, I'm really scared. I could be arrested for murders I didn't commit or be killed myself.'

Penelope started to cry and Richard put his arms around her. She looked up at him and felt just as she had all those years ago.

'Why did you leave me with Arthur, Richard? You knew he didn't love me. I've been so unhappy. I've never stopped thinking about you.'

'I'm sorry, Penelope. I didn't think I could offer you enough.'

'Perhaps not material things,' she replied. 'But they wouldn't have mattered.'

'Yes they would, darling. You're used to having everything you want. As it was, I did very well for myself in the end. It's ironic how things turn out.'

'I'll leave Arthur now, I will,' Penelope said. 'We can be together.'

'We'd better let the police find the murderer first; otherwise they'll be saying we planned the whole thing together.'

Richard stroked Penelope's face, thinking how vulnerable and afraid she seemed to be. Everything was a mess and he wondered who did kill Donald. He couldn't believe Penelope was the murderer. She was much too soft and kind to commit such a crime. It must have been Arthur after all, but he and Donald had always been close, so perhaps it had been Penelope after all. As he looked at her face, he wondered if there was a ruthless woman hiding underneath that gentle exterior. Perhaps she had wanted Arthur to inherit all of Donald's money. After all, she did enjoy the good life. No, he was going crazy and had to pull himself together. Penelope didn't have a nasty bone in her body. The killer could easily be someone from outside the family. Who knew what nasty secrets Donald Forbes had? Richard finally decided that he had thought enough about the murders. He reached down and touched Penelope's lips lightly with his. She smiled and then started to respond. As they began to kiss more passionately, they both realised the spark between them was still very strong. Richard could hardly believe it when Penelope took his hand and led him into the bedroom.

10

Jacqueline woke at seven on the morning of the sail past feeling excited about the day ahead. She had never taken part in one of these events and was looking forward to experiencing it with Will, although she now wished they were going without Jeff.

Like the Forbes, Jacqueline had heard nothing else about the murders, but she had gone to see her parents in Suffolk on Friday afternoon and hadn't arrived back until late on Saturday. She had scanned the Internet and bought a paper for the last few days, but hadn't discovered any new information.

Jacqueline jumped out of bed, quite unusual for her on a weekend morning. She decided to have breakfast at home and after coffee and toast, had a bath and got ready, taking great care over her make-up. She wanted to look good for

Will, admitting to herself that she was a little nervous about seeing him again. What if he had changed his mind about her?

Around nine Jacqueline heard someone knocking at her door and went to answer it. She hoped it was Will, but was disappointed. However, she smiled as she opened the door.

'Liz, how nice to see you. Come in.'

'Hello. I only wanted to make sure you were back safely and were ready for the sail past. Tony Hunter is almost having a breakdown, although I can't imagine why. We all have to sail past him and salute, so it's much harder for us than him. His boat just has to stay still!'

'He's probably worried we'll all do it wrong and show him up.'

'Yes, it wouldn't surprise me if that's what he's concerned about, especially with our M.P. coming. Have you heard? She's sailing on Daniel's boat and it's put Kate's nose right out of joint. I think she's going to sail with Tony; that is as long as she puts on some decent clothes. He won't want her wearing a short skirt and a low cut top.'

'No, he certainly won't,' Jacqueline replied, smiling. 'Mind you, I expect John's upset that she's not sailing with him. I would have thought she would, if only to make Daniel jealous. Really, those two act like a couple of teenagers.'

'I haven't seen John, but I would imagine he's not a happy man. He used to be so pleasant before he met Kate,' Liz said, and then paused for a moment. 'Talking about the sail past, do you want to come with us on our boat?'

'I'm sorry, but I've already accepted an invitation from Will.'

'Really . . . so I take it your date went well?' Liz asked, looking surprised.

Liz was still slightly suspicious of Will's motives, but thought it was best not to say anything else. Most people didn't like others interfering in their love lives and she did want to keep

Jacqueline as her friend. However, she was still going to keep an eye on Will. Jacqueline was vulnerable and she didn't want to see her get hurt.

'I don't know if it was a proper date, but it was a lovely evening,' Jacqueline replied, smiling gently. 'Will was a perfect gentleman, the play was wonderful and I thoroughly enjoyed myself.'

Liz grinned. Perhaps Will was okay. After all, she was only repeating what other people had said about him.

'Are Penelope and Arthur coming for the sail past?' Jacqueline asked, wanting to change the subject.

'No, but Penelope did say she'd be back today for a drink in the bar afterwards. She said Arthur wasn't coming, which is a relief. He's such a miserable man. He's not speaking to her after what he calls 'that fiasco' earlier in the week. Poor Penelope. She's quite a nice woman once you get to know her, isn't she? I think it's just Arthur holding her back.'

'Yes, you're right. He's suffocating

her,' Jacqueline agreed. 'You know, I keep thinking of Richard. I bet he was really handsome and romantic. I'm sure he swept Penelope off her feet.'

Both women became quiet, imagining Penelope with another man. Liz finally interrupted the silence.

'Well, this is no good. Can't stand here all day. I'd better get back and finish cleaning the boat. Frank will think I'm skiving off! I'll see you in the bar after the sail past.'

'Okay. I'd better go and see if Will needs any help.'

She grabbed a jacket in case it got chilly out on the river and went over to Will's boat. Approaching it, she saw two men sitting on deck having coffee.

'Hi there,' Will shouted.

'Hello, I thought you'd be busy cleaning.'

'All done,' Will said. 'We worked hard yesterday so we could have fun today. Hop on board. Have you met Jeff?'

'No, I don't think we know each other. Hello.'

'Hi,' Jeff said. 'I believe you're the girl who first saw the body in the river.'

'Yes, that's me unfortunately,' Jacqueline replied, smiling. 'It came as a bit of a shock.'

'I can imagine.'

'Morning,' a loud voice boomed from the boat on the other side of the pontoon.

Janet emerged, followed by two other women and a man.

'These are some of my old friends from the force, June, Len and Alison. Paul and David are still asleep. They'll have to get up soon if they don't want to sleep through the sail past!'

'Pete was keen on taking the wheel, so perhaps we should go and wake him up,' one of the women said.

'Well, I'm not too sure about that,' Janet remarked. 'He was plastered last night and I don't know if I trust him with my boat. Come on, let's go to the bar and get a quick breakfast. If you see anyone emerge, will you tell them where we are Will?'

Not waiting for a reply, Janet got off her boat with the others in tow.

'She hasn't even bothered to ask if we'll be here or if we're going to the bar for breakfast,' Jeff groaned. 'I bet she'd be put out if she saw us walk in. I've a good mind to do that. That woman has a nerve. I don't know how you put up with her boat being next door to yours, Will, I really don't.'

'Oh, she's not that bad. She's a bit loud and she does speak her mind, but she doesn't deliberately go out of her way to hurt anyone.'

'Could have fooled me,' Jeff added.

'I wonder if Janet has heard anything more about the murders,' Jacqueline said, eager to talk about the subject. 'She usually knows something we don't.'

'I'm sure she'll tell us if she does,' Jeff remarked. 'She's not a woman to keep secrets.'

'I wonder if the absentee brother, Richard Forbes, has turned up yet,' Will said.

147

'Yes, I've thought about that too.' Jeff added. 'There's been nothing in the papers, however, so I doubt it.'

'The more I think about it, the more unlikely it seems that Richard committed the murders,' Jacqueline said. 'He was the black sheep of the family, so I presume he wouldn't inherit anything.'

'But why was Kevin murdered?' Jeff asked.

'Who knows,' Will replied. 'Everybody seems to think he knew something he shouldn't. That does seem to be the most likely explanation. He probably saw the killer murder Donald and then he started blackmailing the murderer. Anyway, let's forget about all this for today. I'm sure the police are much further forward in their investigations than they've let on. We're supposed to be having fun today, not solving crimes. How about bacon sandwiches before we get going?'

Jeff and Jacqueline both nodded, even though Jacqueline thought that solving murders was just as much fun as going on the sail past.

★ ★ ★

Forty-five minutes later the marina sprang to life. Jacqueline was excited, realising that it was almost time for them to go. Tony and Lucy Hunter were naturally the first to leave as they had to position their boat on the river for the other boats to sail past and salute. Jacqueline wondered why the marina held this occasion every year. It was a strange old-fashioned custom and seemed outdated, but Jacqueline liked it when traditions were kept. She thought about the people who would have taken part in sail pasts years ago. They would have been dressed differently and their boats wouldn't have been the same, but they would have all sailed past the commodore and saluted as they were going to do today.

As Tony's boat left the pontoon, Jacqueline noticed his nautical outfit and saw how sparkling clean his boat was. It wasn't surprising as Will said he had been working on it all day on Saturday. Lucy was dressed in what looked like a very expensive suit and she was wearing a hat. Tony was out to make a good impression, but Jacqueline doubted if many other people were taking the sail past as seriously as the Hunters were.

The next boat to leave was Daniel's, with Margaret Parsons, the M.P., on board. The boat passed very close to Will's and Jacqueline managed to have a good look at Margaret. She was tall, with perfectly cut short blonde hair and beautifully done makeup. Jacqueline knew she was in her mid-forties, but she could easily have been a few years younger. There were a couple of other people on the boat as well and Jacqueline imagined they were part of Margaret's staff. She also noticed a man holding a camera who might have been from the local press.

Jacqueline wondered how Kate was

holding up, thinking she was probably still pretty angry. Not being the type of woman to keep anything inside, Daniel wouldn't escape lightly from this humiliation. While she had accepted that John and Kate were childish, Jacqueline couldn't understand how Daniel could get involved in such a stupid game.

Frank and Liz went out next and waved to people standing on the bank on the other side of the marina. Then Janet and her friends came rushing back to their boat, having just finished their breakfast, and shouted to Will to go before them. Will started to untie the ropes, but just before they were about to leave, Jacqueline noticed John's boat coming up and immediately saw Kate. It was quite a warm day, but not as sunny as it had been. Kate had on a pair of very short shorts, a tiny boob tube and high heels. Jacqueline shook her head, thinking how ridiculous she looked and how cold she might get out on the river. However, Jacqueline wasn't surprised to see Kate with John again, knowing their history. Also, seeing the way she was dressed, she imagined Kate had argued with her brother again for wearing so little and he had refused to let her sail on his boat.

Jacqueline felt slightly guilty about having nasty thoughts about Kate. Jacqueline was a kind person, but she did find Kate lacking in style. Kate was a pretty girl, so why did she ruin her looks in such a way?

John looked towards Will's boat and frowned, but Jacqueline waved and Kate called to them.

'Hello, you lot. What a lovely day. See you all in the bar later on.'

'Good grief,' Jeff said. 'That woman doesn't know how to dress at all does she? Can't imagine what John sees in her, can you Will?'

'Well, she is quite pretty, but you're right, she certainly hasn't got any dress sense. I'm not surprised Daniel wouldn't let her sail on his boat. She doesn't suit his image, does she? He certainly wouldn't have wanted a photo of him in the local paper with her; and imagine what Margaret Parsons would have thought.'

Jacqueline was now feeling all out of sorts. Apart from still feeling bad about her negative thoughts towards Kate, she was upset that John hadn't waved. What Kate did or how she dressed was none of her business or anyone else's for that matter, but she and John were friends, so why hadn't he acknowledged her? He couldn't have been upset that she was with Will, could he? That man was truly mixed up. He was in love with Kate, but every time she turned to Daniel, John turned to her. The whole situation was very odd and it suddenly dawned on her that perhaps John might have some mental problems. He didn't seem particularly stable at all. However, Will's boat then started to move and she decided to forget about John and Kate. She wanted to enjoy the day. After all, she was spending it with a much nicer man.

A few minutes later, Jeff brought Jacqueline a glass of wine and she sat down, while Will started to steer the boat out of the marina. Pauline and Sam's narrow boat followed behind them and then Janet brought up the rear. It was going to be a very enjoyable Sunday thought Jacqueline as she took a sip of Chardonnay, all thoughts of John Stevens having left her mind.

11

A couple of hours later Tony Hunter turned his boat around on the Thames to return to his berth in the marina. The commodore was feeling smug, believing he had held a very successful sail past. Knowing that some of the boaters didn't take things like this seriously, he had been certain that somebody would let him down, but it had all gone smoothly and he was sure that Margaret Parsons, the M.P., had been impressed by the occasion. He had sent an invitation to her personally and couldn't believe it when she had accepted. He had to make sure that the press photographer took a photo of himself with Margaret for the local paper. As always, Lucy had put on a good front as the wife of the commodore, but in reality she had found the whole event extremely boring and wondered what the point of it all had been. Now, to make matters worse, she had to spend the rest of the afternoon in the bar being sociable with a very rowdy crowd. She was sure many of them only took part in the sail past for the free punch and buffet afterwards.

Meanwhile, Arthur Forbes was boarding his cruiser in the marina, noticing that many boats were still out on the river. He poured himself a large whisky and sat down trying to get comfortable. He knew he had a difficult afternoon ahead of him, but it needed to be done and he just wanted to get it all over with. Why did he make his life so complicated? It was the last time he was going to do anything like this again, of that he was certain.

Half an hour later, Will and Jeff tied up Will's boat, having told Jacqueline to stay put and finish her glass of wine. She thought back to the sail past, thinking how strange it had all been. Tony and Lucy had sailed a little way up river and stopped. Then all the other boats had sailed past them and saluted the commodore and his wife. They all then sailed further up river until they were past Tony's boat. When the last boat had gone past him, Tony turned his boat around and started to sail back to the marina. The other boats then also turned around and followed him back. Although it seemed a little pointless to Jacqueline, it was traditional and a part of boating life and she had enjoyed it. There was a great deal of camaraderie among the boaters and it was nice being a part of it. Now she was looking forward to the event in the bar. Jim and Cassie had prepared a celebratory buffet and an enormous bowl of punch. She had no doubt that everybody would stay there all afternoon and certain people would get very drunk.

The bar was packed when Jacqueline and Will arrived and she had a problem to see who was there and who wasn't. It seemed as if everybody from the marina, even those who hadn't taken part in the sail past, had come up to the café bar. They clinked glasses, enjoying their punch and then they dug into the buffet. Tony was proud of the sail past and continually posed for photos, but Lucy tried to dodge the cameras. Jacqueline noticed that John kept his eyes continually on Kate, but despite sailing with him she now tried to avoid his gaze. Margaret Parsons stayed for a glass of punch and a bite to eat and while she was there Kate avoided Daniel, but once she left, Kate started hovering around him. Daniel didn't seem to mind, but John looked angry. Jacqueline was fed up with the whole situation. Daniel seemed to fool around with both Kate and John's emotions and it wasn't right. John seemed to be such an intelligent man, except where Kate was concerned. He was making an idiot of himself, but he didn't realise it and Kate was just using him. Perhaps she should talk to Daniel, but he would probably tell her to mind her own business and it could jeopardise her berth in the marina. It was best not to interfere, but John had involved her in the situation by inviting her out and she felt as if she had a right to say something.

★ ★ ★

While this was all going on in the café bar, Arthur heard a knock on his door and then a woman came in without waiting to be invited.

'I take it nobody saw you?' Arthur asked, his voice sounding slightly harsh.

'Of course not. I'm much too clever for that,' she said, going over to kiss Arthur. 'Anyway, it's so packed up there. You can't tell who's there and who's not.'

Arthur moved his lips away from her and she frowned, but didn't say anything about his refusal to kiss her.

'Do you mind if I make a coffee?' she asked. 'I've had a lot to drink and I need to clear my head.'

'Feel free. I'll have one too while you're at it. I've had a couple of whiskies and I'll need a bit to sober up a bit before I drive home.'

The woman went to put the kettle on.

'We need to talk,' Arthur said.

'That sounds ominous,' the woman replied, trying to smile.

'Look, I know you killed Donald and Kevin and I expect you're going to kill Penelope next. I can't live with a murderer. We're finished.'

'What?' the woman said, trying to keep her voice calm. 'How can you say that? How could I have killed them? And more important, why would I have killed them? You're crazy. If I were going to kill anyone, it would have been Penelope. Then we could have been together. But there would have been no need to kill her. You said you were going to divorce her.'

'I've been thinking about it all,' Arthur said, without any emotion in his voice. 'First we'll talk about Donald. Well, you killed him so I would be even richer. You like money, don't you dear?

You resent the fact that if I left Penelope, I would have to give her a great deal of money to get rid of her. So you killed Donald so I would inherit his money. He has no family and has left everything to me.'

Arthur paused as the kettle boiled.

'Make the coffee. I think you'll need it,' he said sharply.

The woman got up, looking pale, and started to make the coffee.

'I need my sweeteners from my bag. Do you want some or are you having sugar again?' she asked, still just about able to keep her voice calm.

'I'll indulge you for the last time and have sweeteners. Penelope doesn't care what I look like, so I'll be able to eat and drink what I want from now on.'

'And drop dead from your arrhythmia or diabetes in a couple of years' time. I'm really surprised you haven't had a heart attack.'

'Any of those would be better than being killed by you, darling.'

'I would never kill you. I love you

more than anybody I've ever loved.'

'Yes, you probably do, but money would probably overcome that one day. Anyway, back to the murders,' Arthur said, taking a sip of coffee. 'God, these sweeteners are horrible. Now, what about Kevin? Shall I take a guess; was he blackmailing you as well? He saw us kissing and decided to get what he could out of it. He blackmailed me, but that wasn't enough, so he started on you? But you couldn't afford to pay him like I could, so you decided to kill him. Nobody liked him, so you thought it wouldn't matter. You thought nobody would miss him. He was just a horrible little man.'

'How do you know if anyone misses him?' the woman said. 'He could have family somewhere that does miss him. You're a cruel person, Arthur.'

Arthur took another sip of coffee and started to feel strange.

'Me, cruel? Even now you're denying everything. You really are evil, aren't you?' Arthur said and then paused, putting his hands to his head.

'Are you alright, Arthur?'

'Have you put something in this coffee? I feel a bit odd?'

'Odd? How, dear?'

'My head hurts and I feel sick. You've gone all blurry as well.'

Arthur tried to stand up, but he couldn't. Suddenly, he was sick.

'Come on dear, let's get you lying down.'

'What've you done?' Arthur slurred, as the woman helped him onto his bed. 'I need water, my mouth's all dry.'

She didn't bother to get him any water.

'Where am I?' he said, his eyes closing.

The woman felt his pulse. It wasn't very strong and she felt it getting even weaker. Smiling, she got up, turned on some music and washed the cups. Then she wiped everything she had touched.

An hour later, back in the bar, Jacqueline looked around for Penelope. She saw Janet standing at the bar and went over to her.

'I was certain Penelope, if not Arthur, was going to come for a drink this afternoon. Did you knock at the Forbes' boat before coming here?'

'No,' Janet answered. 'I completely forgot, sorry.'

'That's okay. I'll nip up and see if she's there. If Arthur hasn't come with her, she might be a bit nervous about coming to the bar on her own,' Jacqueline said.

She walked out of the bar, quite relieved to get a bit of fresh air. She was enjoying herself, but there were a lot of people in the bar and it was getting stuffy.

'Hey, wait for me,' Janet shouted. 'I need something from my boat. I'll walk up with you.'

They got to Janet's boat first, so she went on board, saying she'd wait for Jacqueline. The Forbes' boat was a couple of pontoons further along and just as Jacqueline climbed on board, she noticed a black swan again.

'Hello you,' she said. 'You are a

beautiful bird. Truly magnificent.'

However, she shivered, remembering the last time she had seen a black swan. A few minutes after it had glided past her boat, she had seen the body of Donald Forbes floating behind it. Nervously, she looked up and down the water, but to her relief there wasn't anything to be seen apart from a couple of ducks and moor hens.

Jacqueline knocked at Penelope's door, but there was no reply. However, she thought she could hear music coming from inside, so she tried the handle. To her surprise it opened so she slowly entered the boat.

'Hello, is anyone there? It's just Jacqueline. Penelope, are you here?'

The music seemed to be coming from the bedroom. Jacqueline saw that the door to it was open, so she slowly walked towards it. Once inside, she looked around and suddenly gasped. Arthur was lying on the bed.

'Oh, I'm so sorry.' she said quietly.

Jacqueline turned to leave, but she

had a feeling that something wasn't quite right. She stopped, her heart beating fast. Arthur was very still. She slowly moved towards him and then looked closer, wondering what was wrong. Was he dead or was he only in a very deep sleep? Perhaps he had taken sleeping tablets, but it was a bit early in the day for that. She didn't want to touch him, but what was she to do? Then she remembered that Janet was on her boat. Jacqueline rushed out on deck and shouted.

'Janet, Janet, are you still there?'

'Yes, I am. What is it? I'm a bit busy here.' she said crossly.

Jacqueline couldn't imagine what she was busy doing. After all she had just popped out to get something in the middle of the party.

'It's Arthur. I think he's dead or in a coma or something awful.'

Jacqueline was trembling and almost in tears. Janet's face fell and her voice became gentler.

'Stay there. I'll be with you in a tic.

Don't touch anything.'

Within a couple of minutes, Janet was with Jacqueline and they went into the bedroom together. Janet confirmed that Arthur was still breathing, but it was very shallow. Jacqueline was relieved that Janet was there to take over. She rang for an ambulance and the police and the two women sat out on deck waiting.

'Are you alright?' Janet asked Jacqueline.

'Yes, I think I'm getting used to this now,' Jacqueline said, with a wry grin on her face. 'If you ever can get used to it. You can't really, can you?'

'No, it's not that easy,' Janet replied. 'I know I come over as tough, but I never did think of dead or injured bodies as part of a day's work. Especially if it was a child. That was particularly difficult.'

The two women sat quietly for a while waiting for the police, while the black swan floated past again. Jacqueline shivered.

'Just as I got on the boat, that black

swan came by as one did before I saw Donald's body. I'm beginning to think it's an omen of death.'

'Ah, a superstitious person.'

'You're not then?'

'Nope, but if you see it again and find another body or someone hurt, I could be convinced.'

Jacqueline smiled, but inside she was scared. This was all getting too much now. The Black Swan Marina was becoming a dangerous place to be, but she didn't know anything, so why should she be afraid? The murders didn't have anything to do with her.

'Ah, here they come,' Janet remarked.

Jacqueline turned round and saw Detective Jameson with some other officers.

'Good afternoon,' he said. 'How come I'm not surprised to see you two here? Which one of you discovered Arthur? Or was it both of you?'

'It was me,' Jacqueline said nervously, wondering what he would think of her finding Arthur.

'This is becoming a bit of a habit, Mrs. Lawrence, isn't it? May I ask what you were doing here?'

'Penelope Forbes said she was coming to the bar for a drink after the sail past. She didn't turn up, so I came to see if she was on her boat. I knocked, but got no reply. However, I heard music coming from the boat and when I tried the door, I found it open, so I went in. However, instead of finding Penelope, I found her husband instead. He was on his bed and I thought he was dead though I wasn't certain, so I called Janet.

'And where were you?'

'I was on my boat. I had walked down from the bar with Jacqueline to get something, so don't get any ideas that I had anything to do with the murder.'

'Nothing would be further from my mind, Janet,' Detective Jameson exclaimed. 'So, has nobody seen Penelope?'

'I don't think so,' Jacqueline replied. 'We haven't, anyway.'

'We need to get someone over to her house in London. Now, here are the paramedics. You two women, stay put.'

'I don't think he likes us much,' Jacqueline whispered to Janet.

'It's not you, it's me. He reckons I want to take over the case. As if I could. I'm retired. Mind you, I bet I could solve this quicker than that lot of incompetents.'

Jacqueline had to stifle a laugh, especially as there was still a police officer standing close by who had probably heard her.

'Shush, he might hear you.'

'What of it. They have no idea what they're doing. I'm sure of it.'

'So, what's your take on the case?' Jacqueline whispered. 'Do you think it's the missing brother, Richard, or do you think its Penelope?'

'Oh, Richard of course. Penelope is a dear. She couldn't kill a fly. She's been living under the thumb of that awful husband of hers for years.'

'But what can Richard hope to gain?'

Jacqueline asked. 'Penelope will inherit nearly everything. It doesn't make sense.'

'I would imagine he intended to wait an appropriate length of time till everything had settled down and then come back and woo Penelope,' Janet replied 'He'll be surprised if Arthur makes a full recovery.'

'Arthur wasn't coming down today. It's a bit strange that he's here and Penelope isn't.'

'Yes. Where is Penelope? Now that is a question I can't answer. It doesn't make sense,' Janet said.

Jacqueline was confused as well and was beginning to think there might be a completely different explanation to this series of murders. After all, if it were Richard, he would have to be completely certain that Penelope was still in love with him. Otherwise she could turn him in. The only way it could be Richard was if Penelope had already seen him and they had planned it together. And what about Kevin? No,

Janet's solution to the crimes was flimsy.

'Right,' Detective Jameson said. 'You two are free to go now.'

'He wasn't shot was he?' Janet asked. 'What do you think it was? Poison? A woman's touch.'

'We'll know later,' Detective Jameson said abruptly.

He hated other people interfering in his cases. Ex-police officers were particularly bad, especially this one, and amateur sleuths weren't much better, although Mrs. Lawrence only seemed to be showing a healthy interest in the case and didn't seem to be doing anything reckless. He hoped she would continue in this way, as he wouldn't like any harm to come to her. He imagined she'd had a very hard time the last year and a half since losing her husband.

Janet and Jacqueline walked back to the bar.

'I'm pretty sure it was poison of some sort,' Janet said. 'I couldn't see anything else on his body, not that I looked in too much detail.'

'What are you thinking? That Penelope might have been involved? I thought you didn't think she could kill anyone?'

'I didn't, but perhaps I was wrong. Or perhaps, heaven forbid, that Richard has another female accomplice.'

Jacqueline was dumbfounded.

'You mean, he's going to marry Penelope for all that money, eventually kill her and then be with another woman, whoever that is, the one who tried to kill Arthur? That's very complicated.'

'People will go to a lot of trouble for that much money.'

'I suppose you're right.'

It seemed a bit farfetched to Jacqueline, but she hadn't been involved in murders as much as Janet had. Still, she couldn't see this happening.

By this time, they had reached the bar and Will came rushing up to Jacqueline.

'You've been gone for ages,' he said. 'I've been worried about you.'

'We saw the police go up a little while ago,' Tony remarked. 'No more murders I hope?'

'Unfortunately, possibly,' Janet's loud voice filled the room.

Everybody became quiet, apart from a couple of gasps.

'Jacqueline went onto the Forbes' boat to see if Penelope was there. She said she was coming to the marina for a drink after the sail past. However, Jacqueline found Arthur in a coma. The police won't admit it, but I think he's been poisoned.'

Nobody said anything for a few moments. Then Daniel spoke mournfully.

'What on earth is this going to do for my business? I'll be ruined.'

'Is that all you can think about,' Jacqueline said, suddenly bursting into tears. 'These people have lost their lives. I've found one of them dead and another in a coma. Nobody has been arrested and all you can think about is your business.'

Will put his arm around her and Liz spoke up.

'Yes, she's right. You really aren't a nice man at all, Daniel. I mean have any of us moved our boats out of this marina yet? I don't think so. Your attitude would make us move more than these murders, I can tell you.'

Frank went and put his arm around his wife who also had started to cry. Tony was getting irritated. His sail past was being ruined by murders and crying women. He had to get it back on track and the only way to do it was to put his hand in his pocket. He didn't want to do it, but he'd have to.

'Look everyone, it's been a bit of a shock for all of us, and a difficult couple of weeks, so Jim, Cassie, have you got enough alcohol to make another bowl of that delicious punch of yours?'

'I think we could do that for you,' Jim said, smiling, and thinking of his profit margins.

The room cheered up at the thought of more punch, that is, except for John. Kate had gone over to console Daniel after his telling off. Although he was the owner of the marina, he would never argue with women in public. Then John looked at Will comforting Jacqueline and he felt a pang of regret. Jacqueline was kind and beautiful and sophisticated. He had enjoyed spending time with her. Why did Kate still have this hold on him? And why was she comforting that awful man?

12

Shortly after, the paramedics took Arthur off his boat and Detective Jameson contacted the police in West London. They were instructed to tell Penelope what had happened to her husband and to bring her to the hospital in Slough. It crossed the detective's mind that she could have been the one to poison Arthur. Most of the regulars had been out on the sail past, so she probably wouldn't have been recognised walking from the car park in the marina to her boat and it also wouldn't have taken her long to get back home. Although he still had no concrete evidence she was still a major suspect in the murders of Donald Forbes and of Kevin. He prayed that Arthur would live and would be able to tell them who had tried to kill him.

Meanwhile, Penelope and Richard

were lying together in bed, holding onto each other tightly. He kissed her forehead and she smiled.

'What are we going to do now?' Penelope asked Richard. 'After today there's no way I can bear to be with Arthur.'

'You're going leave him.' Richard replied. 'I'm not poor anymore. I can give you the life you deserve.'

'You make me sound awful. Like all I want is money.'

'I don't mean to, darling. I know you love me, but you need nice things as well. You're not the sort of person that can live in poverty. You would be miserable and then we'd end up hating each other.'

Penelope cuddled up to Richard. He knew her so well. Life was going to be different from now on and she was excited. However, they had better get up, just in case Arthur came home. She didn't want him to find them like this. He would make their relationship seem sordid when it was nothing of the sort.

'Come on, we'd better get up,' she said to Richard.

'Do we have to?' he replied, pulling her back down again.

However, the doorbell rang and Penelope jumped up.

'Who on earth is that?' she exclaimed. 'It can't be Arthur, unless he's forgotten his key. Stay there, Richard. I'll go and see who it is.'

Penelope put on a robe and went to the door. She looked through the peephole and was shocked to see two policemen standing there. She opened the door slowly, feeling afraid. What on earth had happened now?

'Yes?'

'Mrs. Penelope Forbes?'

'Yes, that's me.'

'I'm sorry to tell you that your husband, Mr. Arthur Forbes, is very ill. He's been taken to Wexham Park Hospital in Slough.'

'What? What's happened?'

'If you would like to get dressed, madam, we'll take you there.'

'No, tell me what's happened,' she screamed.

Richard came down the stairs. He'd very sensibly got dressed quickly.

'What's going on? Can't you see you're upsetting the lady?'

One of the police officers took out a photo.

'Mr. Richard Forbes I believe. We have been looking for you in connection with the murders of Donald Forbes and Kevin Wilson. You will need to come down to the station for questioning.'

'No,' Penelope screamed. 'Someone's tried to kill Arthur. I didn't do it, nor did Richard. We were here. Arthur's in hospital, Richard.'

The next thing they knew, Penelope was on the floor, having fainted. When she woke a few minutes later, she was lying on the sofa and Richard was holding her hand.

'Are you alright, darling?'

'I think so. What's going on?'

'One of the officers has phoned a Detective Jameson and we're both going to the hospital in Slough and then we're being questioned.'

'I'm scared,' Penelope said, tears starting to flow

'Don't be,' Richard said, squeezing her hand. 'I'm here. Go and get dressed and then we'll be on our way.'

★   ★   ★

In less than an hour, Penelope and Richard were at Wexham Park Hospital in Slough, being greeted by Detective Jameson.

'Ah, the elusive long lost brother I believe,' Jameson said.

'That's me, the completely innocent long lost brother.'

'Well, that seems unlikely now doesn't it, seeing as you were found with Arthur's wife while Arthur's lying in there fighting for his life.'

'Can we go in and talk to him?' Richard asked, ignoring Jameson's comments.

'No, he's in a coma.'

'Well,' Richard said. 'Don't you think that when he wakes up from his coma he might be able to tell us who did this to him?'

'It's possible, but the doctors think he might never regain consciousness.'

Penelope got up, having been sitting down during the conversation.

'Can I see my husband please?'

'You may, but I will have to go in with you.'

'Fine,' she replied listlessly.

Penelope wasn't bothered if Detective Jameson accompanied her or not. She didn't love Arthur and had no need to be alone with him. She didn't realise that the detective was going in because he had to make sure that she didn't intend to finish Arthur off.

As they went in Penelope noticed how peaceful her husband seemed, just as if he was asleep. She knew at that moment that she didn't care if he ever woke up again. She felt awful having such thoughts, but Arthur never showed her any affection anymore.

Still, she wouldn't have tried to kill him. How dare they think she would? However, she had such a flimsy alibi and as they suspected Richard as well, she might as well not have an alibi at all. Mind you, who else would have wanted him dead? It wasn't surprising they thought that she or Richard or both of them were the killers.

'So, do they know what it was?' she finally asked. 'What did this to him?'

'Belladonna,' Jameson replied

'Oh, isn't that deadly nightshade?'

'It is. How strange you know what it is.'

'I would imagine most people do,' Penelope said sharply.

'Your husband takes medication for arrhythmia, doesn't he?' Jameson continued, ignoring her tone. 'It's very dangerous to mix belladonna with that type of medication.'

'I didn't know that,' Penelope replied, thinking that he was trying to pin this on her. 'Anyway, I was at home all day, not at the marina.'

'I believe you would have had ample time to get there and back.'

Penelope was getting scared. They were trying to frame her. She just wanted to run away with Richard, far away from all of this, but there was no chance now. What if they didn't find the real murderer? She could end up in jail for crimes she hadn't committed. It didn't bear thinking about.

13

As Jacqueline returned home from work in the middle of the afternoon the following day, she met Janet in the car park.

'Going home?' she asked.

'No,' Janet replied. 'I thought I'd stay here for a few days just in case Penelope needs my help.'

'What's happened to her?' Jacqueline asked. 'I've heard nothing since Arthur was taken to the hospital yesterday.'

'Oh, I spoke to a friend in the force,' Janet continued. 'Penelope was found at home with Richard.'

'Really?' Jacqueline replied. 'Have they been arrested?'

'Well, they were taken to the hospital for Penelope to see Arthur, and now they're helping the police with their enquiries. Unfortunately, it does now look as if Penelope's the one who committed the murders. Well, at least been in collusion with her brother-in-law, Richard. They were found in a compromising position at Penelope's home by the way.'

Jacqueline gasped, but she really wasn't that surprised. Arthur treated her terribly, but she still found it hard to believe that Penelope was a cold-blooded killer. No, it couldn't be her. Perhaps she had been part of the plot to kill Donald, Kevin and her husband, but Richard must have been the one to commit the crimes, not her. Still, it was difficult to think she could even have had thoughts of murder.

'How's Arthur by the way?' Jacqueline asked, trying to put all thoughts of Penelope as a killer out of her mind.

'Still in a coma as far as I know,' Janet replied. 'Such a pity. Divorce would have been so much simpler.'

Jacqueline nodded.

'Yes it would. Greed is an awful vice, isn't it? But did Penelope and Richard really think they could get away with it and end up with all the money. They're the most likely suspects, aren't they? I can't believe Penelope would be that naïve.'

'I expect they hoped they would be able to cover their tracks well enough,' Janet said, pausing. 'Well, I'm afraid I can't stop and talk for much longer. I'll see you later. I have lots of errands to run.'

Jacqueline watched Janet leave, feeling a bit down in the dumps. She was just getting to like Penelope and now she could be locked up. However, Jacqueline still wasn't certain that Penelope was the killer. She even doubted that Richard was. As Janet said, divorce would have been much simpler. Murder was always a huge risk, and if you were caught, that was the end of your new life. Jacqueline was so deep in thought that she didn't notice John walking towards her until he was almost standing next to her.

'Good afternoon,' he said coldly.

'Oh, hello,' she replied, ignoring his

tone. 'I hope you enjoyed the sail past yesterday.'

'It was alright. I could see you were having a good time out there on Will's boat.'

Jacqueline wondered why John sounded so cross. Was he playing games again? Why did he have to be so childish? Although they had spent some time together, he had never expressed any romantic feelings towards her and now he sounded as if he were jealous of her relationship with Will. He was a hard man to understand and he could be quite unpleasant at times. She thought again that he might have some sort of mental problems, but then she dismissed these thoughts. It was nothing to do with her if he had. She had been having a lovely time with Will and she realised she was missing him already. She didn't want to waste time brooding over John and his problems. However, she thought she should continue talking to him in the hope of lightening his mood. Jacqueline hated being rude or unpleasant to anyone.

'Yes, Will's boat is lovely,' she said. 'It's a pity the afternoon ended so terribly.'

John felt slightly guilty, realising what a shock it must have been for her to find Arthur. Jacqueline was certainly having a run of bad experiences.

'I'm sorry that happened. It must be putting you off living at The Black Swan Marina.'

'No, not really. I mean, it was awful, but I still love it here. I've made so many good friends and I do feel comfortable living here. I think the murders all revolve around the Forbes family anyway, so none of us have anything to worry about. Mind you, I still can't work out were Kevin fits into it all.'

'You're probably better off not knowing. It could put your life in danger.'

Jacqueline frowned. What made him say that? Did he know something? But she just shook her head and decided it was time to end the conversation. She was feeling awkward with him and didn't feel that her efforts to make him feel relaxed were working.

'Anyway, I'd better go,' Jacqueline said quickly. 'I'll see you later.'

'Yes, bye,' John said abruptly and walked away.

He was angry that Jacqueline seemed to want to get away from him and was certain Will was turning her against him.

Jacqueline watched John walk quickly towards the car park and wondered where he was going. She was confused about him and wished he would act normally. One minute he seemed natural and easy to talk to, but the next he put her on edge.

Getting onto her barge, Jacqueline looked over at the Forbes' boat and shivered, remembering the previous afternoon. She wished she could put it out of her mind, but it seemed impossible. She had picked up her mail at the Marina office and hoped that reading it would distract her. She got herself a coffee and started flicking through the letters when she realised there was one from Penelope which had been sent the previous Thursday. Jacqueline trembled as she opened the envelope, pausing for a few minutes before starting to read it.

Dear Jacqueline

By the time you read this, I may be gone. I don't know what is going to happen in the next few days. Richard, Arthur's brother has come back to England and has phoned me. I haven't seen him yet, but I'm going to make sure that Arthur goes to the marina on his own this Sunday and I'll see Richard while he's out. I think I still have feelings for him and I'm sure he's not committing these murders. He was such a wonderful man and would never do anything like this. I think my husband killed both Donald and Kevin. Donald has left him everything in his will. Arthur is greedy you see. As for Kevin, he must have seen Arthur kill Donald. That's the only explanation I can think of. One other thing, I'm sure Arthur is having an affair with someone at the marina. I have no idea who she is, but he's always sneaking out to meet her when we're at the marina and he makes excuses to go to the marina on his own as well. I don't really care. Arthur's so cruel to me you know and I don't love him. If I leave him for Richard, he'll try and stop me getting any money, but he's being unfaithful so that's not right. See if you can find out who she is please. Don't let him get away with it.

Say goodbye to Janet and Liz for me.

Your friend
Penelope

Jacqueline read the letter twice, not knowing what to think. This put a whole new perspective on the case and perhaps Richard had nothing to do with it at all. Perhaps Arthur had killed both Kevin and Donald, but then who had tried to kill Arthur? Perhaps it was the husband of the mistress? Or perhaps it was the mistress for some reason. Possibly Arthur had tried to end the affair. Now who could she be? Jacqueline hardly thought it was Janet. She was too loud and boorish for Arthur. She also didn't think it could be Cassie. Cassie and Jim seemed happy and in love and anyway, she wouldn't have much opportunity. The bar was open such long hours. She also didn't think it could be her friend, Liz, who seemed happy with her husband Frank. Then there was Pauline next door. Perhaps it could be her. Sam and Pauline's marriage seemed fine, but they didn't seem head over heels in love. Lucy Hunter, the wife of the commodore would be highly unlikely to have an affair, but then perhaps she had a wild side and envied her sister in law, Kate. And, yes, Kate, now she was crazy about men and Jacqueline could see her having an affair with anyone. She could have turned Arthur's head with her short skirts and low cut tops. Kate loved money and Arthur could have showered her with gifts.

Jacqueline phoned Detective Jameson and he was on her barge within half an hour. He read the letter three times and then nodded. Jacqueline wished he'd say something.

'So, what do you think?' she asked impatiently.

'Well,' he said, nodding again.

He knew he shouldn't really go into too much detail with her, but she was an intelligent woman and thought she was also discreet.

'Well, this does open the case a little. Penelope is a major suspect, but if there is a mistress, she would also be a suspect, as could be the husband. Of course, the letter could just be a red herring.'

'I thought of that too,' Jacqueline said. 'If there is a mistress why would she want to kill Arthur?'

'He could have ended the relation-ship with her and made her angry. As I said, poison is often used by women.'

'So it was poison.'

'Yes . . . '

Jacqueline was getting more and more intrigued, but thought it best not to pry any more.

'So, what will you be doing now?' was all she asked.

'I shall interview as many women at the marina as I can, though I'm sure none of them will admit having an affair with Arthur. Is this copy of the letter for me?'

'Yes, of course.'

Jacqueline's printer had a photocopy-ing application on it.

A few moments later, Jacqueline showed Detective Jameson out and then poured herself a glass of wine. She was getting very excited by the turn of events.

Half an hour later, there was a knock at the door and she answered it to find Janet and Will standing there. Her heart missed a beat when she saw him, and with her adrenalin still pumping, all she wanted to do was throw her arms around him and kiss him. Unfortunately, with Janet there, she thought it best to restrain herself.

'Hello you two, come in. Glass of wine?'

Will accepted, but Janet had her usual beer. When they had all sat down, Jacqueline went on to tell them about Penelope's letter. She watched Janet's face.

'Looks like I could have been wrong,' Janet said, sounding disappointed.

'Not necessarily. She could easily have been lying to put the police on the wrong track,' Jacqueline remarked, knowing that Janet hated being wrong.

'Perhaps, but what if she wasn't,' she said, her eyes suddenly lighting up. 'Who on earth do you think Arthur was having an affair with?'

'It did cross my mind it could have been Lucy Hunter,' Jacqueline said.

'Lucy Hunter!' Janet exclaimed.

'Well, it's nearly always the most unlikely person. I mean, she's so prim and proper, but perhaps underneath it all, there's a crazy woman wanting to get out, but Tony won't let her. And then she sees Kate having all this fun and she wants some of it.'

Will and Janet both laughed.

'You know, you could be right!' Janet exclaimed.

There was another knock at the door and Will answered it. This time it was Liz.

'Liz, hello,' Jacqueline said. 'Not going back home again this week?'

'No, I've been offered the job in the chandlery and I've accepted. Frank's okay with it, especially as we could do with the extra money.'

'Oh, that's great. It will be lovely to have you here more often,' Jacqueline said. 'Glass of wine?'

'Yes, please,' Liz said.

'All this alcohol is making me hungry,' Will remarked. 'Shall we get a take out? Indian perhaps?'

They all agreed and while Will went to get the food, Jacqueline and Janet brought Liz up to date with the latest news on the murders.

14

On Tuesday Penelope and Richard were released from police custody as there wasn't enough evidence to hold them. Arthur still remained in a coma in hospital and Penelope was allowed to see him with a police officer present. She wasn't particularly keen on visiting, but felt it would look suspicious if she didn't go to the hospital.

Detective Jameson started interviewing the women at the Black Swan Marina, but most of them only came down to their boats at weekends so it was a laborious task finding them. As predicted, nobody would admit to having any romantic interest in Arthur whatsoever and Jameson was no further forward in discovering the elusive mistress.

John Stevens had left his boat on Monday afternoon to return to his house in Farnham Common. Kate wasn't going to be at the marina until the weekend and he didn't want to see Jacqueline with Will. After their last encounter, Jacqueline was relieved that he wasn't around the marina.

Will had to go on an assignment for work in Manchester and Jacqueline wished he wasn't going, even though she knew he would be back in a couple of days' time. She was finding herself thinking about him more and more. As Will was away, Jacqueline spent time with Liz in the evenings, which helped keep her mind off Will a little.

On Wednesday afternoon, having just returned home from work, Jacqueline's mobile rang. It was Liz.

'Are you at home?'

'Yes,' Jacqueline replied. 'I've just got in.'

'Great,' Liz said, sounding pleased. 'Can you come to the chandlery? I've found a letter. It's a bit faded, but you can just about make it out. Will you come and have a look? I think it might be really important.'

Jacqueline was intrigued and dashed up to the chandlery.

'Here it is,' Liz said excitedly. 'Take a look.'

Jacqueline started to read.

Darl Kevin

I miss yo . . . Last night was wonder.. When can we m . . .

Don't . . . take . . . .long. If y an to run .I will

With so much l . . . Penel

'Oh my goodness,' Jacqueline exclaimed. 'It's a love letter from Penelope to Kevin. This is getting more and more complicated. Gosh, I can't believe that Penelope could have had an affair with Kevin. He was so unpleasant. This means that the most likely person to kill him would have been Arthur. Then Arthur must have killed Donald for his money. That's the only explanation I can think of.'

'I agree,' Liz said. 'Then do you think Penelope tried to kill Arthur because she suspected he killed Kevin, the man she loved? Which means Arthur didn't have a lover after all.'

'It's possible, though would she have had enough time to get here and back home on the day of the sail past? The police think she would, but I'm not certain. Mind you, Arthur could still have had a lover. Arthur and Penelope's marriage was on the rocks. But then what about Richard? Penelope and Richard were found in bed together later in the day of the sail past, so perhaps Richard did kill Kevin to get him out of the way and then tried to kill Arthur. Look, we'll have to call the police again.'

'Yes, you're right. Do you want to do it or shall I?'

'I will,' Jacqueline said. 'Detective Jameson has left me his mobile number. I think he reckons that after I found Donald and Arthur, I might find something or someone else!'

Jacqueline had brought her bag with her and took out her mobile.

'Well,' she said a few minutes later. 'Detective Jameson is coming over as soon as he can. He sounded very interested.'

'So you still think Arthur may have been having an affair?' Liz asked Jacqueline as they waited for Detective Jameson.

'Yes, that's still a possibility. What do you think?'

'I don't know, but I still can't think who he was having an affair with at this marina,' Liz replied. 'He wasn't exactly the most gorgeous looking man around. Well, you could forgive that if he had a personality, but he didn't even have that.'

'My goodness, that was said with a bit of venom,' Jacqueline said.

She was surprised to hear Liz speak in such a way. It was so out of character.

'I'm sorry,' Liz said quickly. 'You know Frank and me; we try to make everyone welcome. We invited Arthur and Penelope for dinner on our boat a while back and they came. Penelope was fine. Well, she tried to be. He kept putting her down, disagreeing with everything she said. I could see she was miserable with him. Good for her if she did have an affair with Kevin, not that he was much better than Arthur, but some women do seem to choose the same type of man. Penelope deserved someone so much better.'

Jacqueline nodded. She knew she had been lucky to have had such a wonderful husband and even if she didn't meet anyone else again, it wouldn't matter. Then she thought of Will. Despite such a shaky start, he really was getting under her skin. Every time she thought of him, she shivered. Liz had been wrong about him. He was absolutely wonderful and she couldn't wait to see him again. She then thought about John. Initially she had been slightly attracted to him, but that had just been because he reminded her of her husband. The more she had got to know him, the more afraid she was of him. He was unstable and nothing at all like Jonathon. She shivered a little, remembering how he had frightened her the other day.

A knock at the door disturbed her thoughts and she went and let in Detective Jameson.

'Come in,' Jacqueline said.

'Good afternoon, ladies. I believe you've found an interesting letter, Mrs. Boyle, indicating that Penelope Forbes and Kevin Wilson were having a relationship.'

'Yes,' Liz replied. 'I'm running the chandlery now and I was cleaning in the back and I found this.'

Detective Jameson studied the letter for a few moments.

'Well, this does put another slant on the case. I'll take it with me if you don't mind.'

'Of course,' Liz replied.

'Any news about Arthur coming out of his coma?' Jacqueline asked.

'Not yet, I'm afraid.' Jameson replied. 'Unfortunately, the longer he stays like this, the less likely it is he'll wake up.'

'If he did, he might be able to tell us

who did this to him,' Liz added.

'Yes, you never know. We'll just have to hope,' the detective said.

Jacqueline and Liz both looked at him and said nothing. Jacqueline shivered, a sense of foreboding flooding over her. She was certain that this hadn't ended yet and that something awful was still going to happen.

'Well, I'll be on my way now,' Detective Jameson said. 'Be careful both of you.'

'Well, he's certainly made me feel a bit creepy,' Liz said when he had left.

'Yes, I get the impression that he feels that there are bad things still to come.'

'I promised Frank I'd go home tonight, but if you're feeling a bit nervous, I'll stay here.'

'Don't be silly,' Jacqueline replied. 'I'll be fine, Go and see that husband of yours.'

'Okay. See you tomorrow then.'

Jacqueline went and poured herself a glass of wine and put some music on. She had lived alone for a long time and had never been afraid, but she had to admit that she was a little nervous. However, why would anyone want to kill her? She had done nothing apart from discovering a dead body and a comatose one. She shouldn't be afraid. After a while, Jacqueline fell asleep on her couch, but half an hour later a knock on the door woke her up. She sat up, unable for a moment to remember where she was. Then she heard a voice call out.

'Jacqueline, are you there?'

She jumped up, realising it was Will, and she rushed to the door.

'What are you doing here? I thought you weren't back until tomorrow?'

'Well, that's a nice greeting. I manage to get away early and that's all you can say,' Will joked.

Jacqueline smiled, butterflies filling her stomach. What was wrong with her? She was feeling more nervous with Will today than she had when they went out to the theatre on their first date!

'I'm sorry, I just wasn't expecting you. Of course I'm pleased to see you,' Jacqueline said.

She then decided to throw caution to the wind and she kissed him lightly on the lips, but then moved away quickly. Will grinned and grabbed her, kissing her more passionately, his lips hungry for hers. He was so pleased to be back and to be with Jacqueline again. She was beautiful, but she was vulnerable as well and he wasn't going to overdo it. He wanted to hold her forever, but he couldn't push things. He pulled away gently, taking her hands and leading her to the settee.

'I've just been in the office,' Will spoke gently. 'Daniel said Detective Jameson was here again. Is everything alright?'

Their kiss was still lingering on his lips, but he was worried why the detective had visited.

'Yes, everything is fine. I called Jameson over.'

Jacqueline went on to tell Will what had happened.

'Well, I'd never have believed it,' Will remarked. 'Penelope and Kevin. What an unlikely couple, but then the strangest people can be attracted to each other. And from what we've heard, she wasn't getting on with her husband. But still, Penelope and Kevin. You're sure the letter is genuine?'

'I've not really thought about it, but now you mention it, they would have made a very unlikely couple. Plus, I find it very odd that Kevin hadn't completely destroyed the letters,' Jacqueline continued. 'Not the kind of thing you'd want to leave around. Yes, you could be right; somebody could have planted the letter there.'

'But who?' Will asked.

'I don't know. It just doesn't add up.'

'No it doesn't. I would have thought the police would have scoured the chandlery before now, so the letter should have been found much earlier,' Will remarked, and then paused for a few seconds. 'You're getting very interested in the whole thing, aren't you?'

'I am, I know. There seems to be so

many possibilities as to who the killer could be. It really is exciting.'

Will smiled, thinking how exciting Jacqueline was as well. She was beautiful and full of life, but he was still nervous as to how to conduct a relationship with her. She had been very much in love with her husband and he didn't want to frighten her away by going too fast. However, he needn't have worried.

'Would you like to stay for dinner?' Jacqueline asked. 'It won't be anything special. I'll just rustle up something from the fridge, but I'd quite like a bit of company tonight. That's if you're not doing anything?'

'No, I mean no I'm not doing anything,' Will said quickly. 'I'd love to join you for dinner. I've got a bottle of wine in my fridge. I'll just go and get it.'

'Okay. That would be lovely,' Jacqueline replied, smiling. 'I'll get started on dinner.'

Jacqueline went into the galley. Her fridge and cupboards were pretty full.

She loved to cook and always made sure she had plenty of the things she liked in stock, but what would she make this evening? She didn't know what Will liked to eat. Were his tastes sophisticated or simple? Did he like spicy food? Or perhaps that wasn't the best choice for an early date. What about Italian? That usually went down well with most people. She had to admit she was nervous. While she was pondering, Will returned with the wine.

'There you go,' he said.

'Thanks, would you like a glass now?'

'Wouldn't mind. I'll open it.'

Jacqueline passed him a bottle opener and glasses.

'Is there anything you don't like to eat?'

'No, I love everything,' he said. 'I'm easy to please!'

Jacqueline breathed a sigh of relief and decided to cook her famous chicken cacciatore with potatoes, garlic bread and a rocket salad.

'You go and sit down,' Jacqueline

said. 'Put on some music if you like. I don't mind what you choose.'

Will looked through the CDs. There was quite a mixture of rock, blues and pop. He wondered which she had chosen and which had been her husband's. He hoped he didn't upset her by putting on one of Jonathon's, but she had said to pick any of them. In the end he put on Leanne Rimes, feeling certain that it was one of Jacqueline's choices.

'That was one of Jonathon's favourite singers,' Jacqueline said almost immediately.

'Oh, I'm so sorry,' Will said quickly. 'I can change it if you prefer.'

'Don't be silly. I like it too. Will, you don't have to tip toe around Jonathon, you really don't.'

Will didn't know what to say, so he just nodded. He was finding it difficult. He'd been out with divorced women before and he himself was divorced, but he had never had a relationship with a widow and he felt out of his depth.

However, after a couple of glasses of wine, they managed to both relax and enjoy their dinner.

'So, how long have you been boating, Will?' Jacqueline asked at the end of the meal.

'Oh, I've had boats on and off for twenty years. I love them, but my ex-wife thought they were a waste of money. The girls enjoyed going on them when they were little, but they're bored with them now. They come down occasionally, but they're sixteen and eighteen now and they'd rather be out with their friends.'

'You must miss the girls a lot?'

'Yes, I do. But I suppose I wouldn't see that much of them if I were at home. Janice, my ex-wife, says they're always out. She's always moaning that she never sees them and blames me for not telling them to stay in more. As if they'll listen to an absentee father.'

'Yes, I can imagine it's hard.'

'And you, didn't you want children?'

'No, not really, I'm not the maternal

type I'm afraid.'

'Nothing wrong with that at all.'

'We did have a dog. Unfortunately she died a few months ago. I've been thinking of getting another one. Daniel says it's okay to keep one here.'

'Yes, you should. It would be great company and I'm sure it would make you feel safer with all these murders going on ... Oh, I'm sorry; I didn't mean to make you feel scared.'

'That's alright. I'm not really frightened. These murders are all connected aren't they? I don't think any of us are in any real danger, unless of course we stumble across some evidence. This case seems so complicated. It gives me a headache just thinking about it!'

'Me too. And just imagining either Penelope or Arthur having an affair makes me go all weird!'

'Now now, Will, that's not nice!'

'Nor is the thought of either of them having an affair!'

They both laughed.

'Well, I suppose I should be going

now,' Will said. 'I have to be up really early for work again and I suppose you have to work too?'

'Yes, my first client is at nine tomorrow.'

Jacqueline walked Will to the door and they both stood there awkwardly. Will so wanted to kiss her again, but he didn't know if he should. Would she think he wanted more? He knew she wasn't ready for moving to the next level yet.

Jacqueline looked at Will standing there nervously and she was aware that he wanted to kiss her again. He really was sweet and to think she'd thought he was so sure of himself at first. She had had quite a few drinks and felt quite brave, so as she opened the door and they went out on deck, she took Will's hands and reached up and gently pressed her lips to his. The kiss became more passionate and Will felt his whole body shiver. This was the most amazing woman he had ever met. As their lips parted, he couldn't say anything and he just looked into her beautiful brown eyes.

'Goodnight, Will,' Jacqueline said. 'I've really enjoyed this evening.'

'Me too,' he finally said. 'Goodnight, Jacqueline.'

They smiled at each other and as Will walked along the pontoon, he hoped he could keep in a straight line. However, it wasn't too much alcohol that was making him swerve, but the excitement of that kiss.

On the boat on the next pontoon, John was watching and seething with jealousy. He had become restless at home and had started thinking about Jacqueline. He couldn't stay at home any longer, but had to return to the boat to see her. He had completely forgotten about Kate, having decided that she wasn't a classy woman at all. Jacqueline, on the other hand, was. He remembered preparing dinner for her and wondered how she could have forgotten about that evening and turned to Will so quickly? He didn't remember that his mind had been on Kate that whole evening. Why did women do this to him all the time? He would speak to her tomorrow and sort it out. He and Jacqueline were made for each other. How dare Will interfere?

15

The following morning Jacqueline was walking towards the car park when she heard her name being called from behind. Turning, she saw John.

'Good morning, John, how are you?' she asked.

'All the better for seeing you,' he said smarmily.

Jacqueline was surprised to hear the tone in his voice and wondered why he was speaking to her like that yet again. It was beginning to frighten her and she wondered if she should head towards the office where she would be safe. She imagined what it must be like to have a stalker and she shivered.

'It's been ages since we've spent some time together,' John remarked. 'I was hoping you would have dinner with me soon.'

'Oh,' Jacqueline replied, thinking how

she could let him down gently and not make him angry. 'I'm afraid I have a lot on at the moment. Can I get back to you when I've checked my diary? At the moment I'm running late for my first client.'

John was in no mood to be put off. He'd been up half the night thinking about Jacqueline and how Will had stolen her from him. He'd had enough with Daniel taking Kate away from him and he wasn't going to put up with a repeat performance here.

'We were getting on so well until Will came along,' he said angrily. 'Why won't you give me another chance?'

Jacqueline was stunned by John's remarks. There had been nothing going on between them apart from a vague friendship. Had he fantasised about her in between his liaisons with Kate to the extent that he believed they had a relationship? She had been certain that he was in love with Kate, in fact the whole marina thought he was in love with Kate. John was always jealous and angry whenever she turned her attentions to Daniel and was always over the moon when she came running back to him. Jacqueline was beginning to think that John could be dangerous and she felt concerned, both for herself and for Will. Would he start interfering in their relationship? Would she be able to reason with him? Unfortunately, she didn't think it was possible.

'John, I'm sorry, but we're just friends, that's all. I apologise if you thought there was anything else between us.'

'You will be,' he said and stormed off.

Jacqueline was shaking and was unable to move for a few moments. She didn't know what to do. When she felt able to, she started to walk towards the car, but then decided to stop by the office. Daniel should be there and she wondered if anything similar had happened to Kate. She opened the door and stood there, feeling slightly stupid. Perhaps she had overreacted.

'Good morning, Jacqueline,' Daniel

said. 'Are you alright? You look very pale.'

'I'm . . . Oh, I don't know if I should say anything. I've just had a bit of a nasty experience.'

'Come and sit down before you fall down,' Daniel said.

Jacqueline sat down and Daniel gave her a glass of water. She paused and then decided it would be best to tell him what had happened. She didn't really think John would do anything, but just in case he did, at least someone would know about his threats.

'I'm glad you told me,' Daniel said when she had finished speaking. 'He sometimes spoke like that to Kate, but you know her, she takes things like that with a pinch of salt. So far, he's not done anything, but you never know. I don't think he's all there myself. Got a screw loose or something.'

'Has he ever threatened you?' Jacqueline asked.

'No, he wouldn't dare. I'm the owner of the marina and he wouldn't want to get thrown out, but let me know if he says anything to Will. I doubt if he will do anything, but it pays to be on your guard. Maybe it's time to get that dog of yours!'

'Perhaps you're right,' Jacqueline said, smiling for the first time that morning. 'Anyway, I'll be off to work. Thank you very much for listening.'

Jacqueline got in her car, but as she turned on the ignition, she found herself trembling again. She had liked John when she had first met him. Yes, he was slightly dull, but he had seemed a shy and gentle sort of man who had not been lucky with the opposite sex. However, he had appeared to be completely different this morning. There was a vicious side to him and he had frightened her. She leant her head on the steering wheel as she felt a tear fall. Things had been so much easier with Jonathon. Why did he have to leave her? Suddenly Jacqueline heard banging at her window and she jumped. She looked up and was relieved to see that it was only Janet.

'Are you okay?' Janet asked.

She could see that Jacqueline was upset and despite her gruff exterior, Janet hated to see her friends unhappy.

Jacqueline nodded, but the tears started to fall even more as she opened the window.

'What on earth is wrong?' Janet asked, sounding very concerned.

Jacqueline told her all about her encounter with John.

'You just leave him to me. I'll make sure he doesn't come anywhere near you.'

'No, no, please. It's better left alone. He's the sort of man who would apologise and promise never to be like that again, but then sneak around quietly to take his revenge.'

'If you're sure,' Janet replied. 'Mind you, you're probably right about him. We'll all just keep an eye on him. I always thought there was something odd about him, skulking about and not saying much. Not to mention his unnatural obsession with Kate.'

'I thought he was quite nice at first. How wrong can you be?'

'True. Off to work are you?'

Jacqueline nodded. She felt a bit better having talked to a couple of people. She was probably overreacting and John was probably harmless.

★   ★   ★

The day went quickly enough and when Jacqueline got back to the marina, John's boat looked quiet and there seemed to be no sign of him. She felt relieved. Janet was sitting out on deck with a beer and shouted over to her.

'Haven't seen John all day. Probably knows you've told a few people and is keeping a low profile.'

'Hope so,' Jacqueline called back.

Pauline came out of her boat with a few beers.

'Janet told me about John. Can't believe it. Horrid man.'

Jacqueline smiled. News certainly did

spread around the marina quickly.

'Why don't you come over, Jacqueline,' Janet called out. 'Pauline's coming for a few drinks. Think I've got some wine for you.'

Jacqueline hesitated for a moment. She had planned to just lie down and rest as the confrontation with John had taken a lot out of her. However, being with friends might take her mind off it all.

'Okay. I'll just get changed and I'll be over in a tick.'

Half an hour later, Jacqueline went over to Janet's boat to find that Will was standing on deck. As soon as he saw Jacqueline, he reached out to help her on board. He put his arms around her and kissed her lightly. Janet and Pauline glanced at each other and smiled.

'Jacqueline,' Will said, sounding very concerned. 'Janet's just told me what happened this morning. I've half a mind to go over and tell John what I think of him and to warn him to keep away from you, but the girls have said it's better to leave him to calm down.'

'Yes, let's not encourage him. There's something wrong with that man. It wouldn't surprise me if he's forgotten about this morning anyway and turned his thoughts back to Kate.'

Will was still holding onto Jacqueline and she could feel her heart beating faster than normal. She looked into his eyes and trembled. He was so gorgeous and not only that, he was worried about her. The kisses last night definitely hadn't been a mistake and what really surprised her was that for the first time, she didn't feel guilty. She felt that Jonathon would have approved of her choice. She thought again of the previous evening and how relaxed she had felt. Then, on the spur of the moment, she had kissed Will. He had been taken completely by surprise.

'Where's that wine then, Janet? I'm parched,' Jacqueline asked.

'Oh, yes, I forgot,' Janet replied.

It wasn't often that Janet was quite so lost for words.

Soon Liz joined them and Jacqueline asked if any more clues about Penelope and Kevin's affair had been found in the chandlery.

'Unfortunately not,' she replied. 'The police have been in having a look, but they haven't found anything. I doubt very much if they will.'

'It does seem cut and dried now doesn't it?' Janet said 'Arthur must have killed Kevin because he had an affair with his wife and Donald because he wanted his money. Penelope probably tried to kill Arthur because he killed her lover, Kevin.'

Jacqueline looked doubtful.

'You're not certain?' Janet asked.

'It's the most probable explanation, but I still haven't given up on the idea of Richard being involved.'

'Why would he kill Kevin?' Pauline asked.

'Say Richard came back and met Penelope and they decided to get back together. Kevin found them in a compromising position and threatened to tell Arthur so Richard killed him.'

'What about Donald?'

'I think Arthur probably still killed him, but Richard tried to kill Arthur.' Jacqueline continued. 'Then the plan was that Richard and Penelope would run off together, but with Arthur in a coma, that would make things more complicated. They would want him dead. Perhaps one of them is going to try and sneak into his hospital room and kill him. And then there's Arthur's mistress, if there is one. Oh, I don't know. It all just seems so complicated.'

'It does,' Liz said. 'And I keep thinking there's going to be another murder. I don't know why. It doesn't seem finished.'

'God, I hope you're wrong,' Jacqueline said.

'Me too,' Pauline added.

'Talking about awful things,' Janet said. 'Look who's coming off his boat. I didn't think he was there. It was so dark and quiet.'

Everyone turned and saw John

getting off his boat. He stopped and stared at them. Jacqueline looked at him and for a moment actually felt sorry for him. They had spent a pleasant evening together once, but this morning he had been really spiteful. She thought there must be a story behind that mixed up personality of his. Jacqueline wondered if he was going to say anything, but he didn't. He bowed his head as he walked away.

'Well, that was strange,' Will said. 'He looked scared of us.'

'Probably embarrassed,' Jacqueline remarked. 'I don't think he's a really vicious man. He's just not a lucky person in love and he's probably fed up with it.'

'You're so forgiving, Jacqueline,' Will said smiling. 'I don't know if I would be.'

'I certainly wasn't this morning I can tell you. But, you can't bear grudges. It just eats you up.'

Jacqueline was constantly amazing Will. He realised he was falling head over heels in love with her and he knew he had to pull himself back. He was certain that she wasn't ready and would want their relationship to develop slowly, but he didn't know how he could do it. Since his divorce, he had indulged in flings and hadn't wanted anything serious. He hadn't met anyone he was that interested in until now and all he wanted to do was shower Jacqueline with compliments and kisses and take her to the best places he could afford or even couldn't afford, but he had to slow down and or she might run away scared.

'Hey, do you all fancy going down to the pub for some dinner?' Janet said, disturbing Will's thoughts. 'As we've been drinking, we'd better walk, but it's only ten minutes away. It would make a change from staying round here.'

Will looked at Jacqueline, hoping she'd decline and suggest they spent an evening alone, but she was already agreeing.

'Oh, that sounds like a great idea. I

feel like a night out after today. You'll come too won't you, Will?'

After she had invited him specially, he felt quite happy going, thinking there might still be a chance of a goodnight kiss. Liz and Pauline both agreed to go as well. Pauline phoned Sam who was on his way back from work in London. She told him to meet them in the pub.

They all enjoyed the evening and had lively discussions about the murders, but as usual no conclusions were reached, apart from the decision that the whole thing was very complicated. As they left the pub, Will put his arm around Jacqueline, and to his delight she didn't push him away, but rather moved closer to him. As they got back to the marina, he started to look forward to his goodnight kiss, but as they approached their boats, Janet exclaimed,

'I know I've had a few, but isn't that a boat stuck to the other side of the bank over there. It looks like it's got off its moorings.'

They all rushed over to have a look.

'My God, that's my boat,' Will shouted. 'How on earth did that happen? It was well and truly tied up. I'm not some novice boater you know.'

'We know you're not,' Sam said. 'Someone's untied your boat.'

'And we all know who it was,' Janet spoke loudly. 'It's that John. I mean, who else could it be after the threats he made this morning?'

'I can't believe it,' Jacqueline said, almost in tears. 'I thought he was all talk, but evidently he's not. How could he do that, how could he?'

'Come on, we're all going to confront him,' Janet insisted. 'And then we'll sort out your boat, Will.'

They marched over to John's boat, but despite banging at his door, there was no reply. Janet tried the door, but it was locked.

'Hum, wonder if he's done a runner?' she said.

'A coward, that's what he is,' Liz remarked. 'And to think, I considered him a good friend.'

'Come on,' Sam said. 'Let's get Will's boat back to where it belongs.'

They went over to the other side of the bank, but when they went on board the boat, they were shocked to find that most things inside had been turned upside down and some even broken. Will was stunned and found it hard to comprehend that someone could have done this to his boat. Had anything been stolen as well?

'Right,' Janet said firmly. 'Leave everything as it is. I don't think we should even move the boat for the time being. We'll have to call the police.'

'I'd better do it as it's my boat,' Will said.

He didn't sound angry, just sad that somebody could hate him so much as to do this to him. It had to be John. He hadn't realised what a warped mind that man had. Perhaps he was also involved in the murders in some way. After this, he wouldn't put anything past him. Jacqueline was thinking the same things as him and had become very quiet.

'Hey,' Pauline asked her. 'Are you okay?'

'Not really. I can't believe John could have done this to Will. I'm just hoping he's not done anything to my boat as well.'

'I'm sure he hasn't,' Pauline said. 'We'll check anyway. I expect the police will want to have a look when they find out what he said to you this morning.'

Will, who had gone on deck to call the police, came back.

'Detective Jameson was there and he'll be along shortly.'

'He'll want to move here,' Liz said, almost smiling. 'He's been back and forth to the marina so many times recently!'

Everybody nodded and smiled a little, but nobody felt particularly cheerful. They had had such a lovely evening and now it was ruined. Life had certainly changed at the Black Swan Marina over the last couple of weeks.

Within fifteen minutes Detective Jameson and another officer had arrived and Jacqueline proceeded to tell them of what had happened that morning with John. Afterwards, Jameson let Will move his boat back while he and the other police officer went to see if John was back on his boat. Unfortunately, he was nowhere to be found. They then went over to Jacqueline's barge and to her relief everything was as she had left it earlier.

'We have Mr. Stevens' home address from our earlier investigations, so we'll go there next,' Detective Jameson said. 'However, I doubt if he'll be there, presuming he is the culprit in this charade.'

'I don't know who else you think it can be,' chimed in Janet. 'It's pretty obvious, don't you think?'

Jameson glared at her. Why did that woman have to poke her nose into his cases whenever she got the opportunity? Granted, she had been a good detective, but she was retired and she hadn't got the right to try and take over. He tried to compose himself and ignore her. There was no point in arguing as she always thought she was right. Instead, he turned towards Jacqueline.

'If I were you, Mrs. Lawrence, I would stay with one of these other ladies tonight, just to be safe.'

'Oh, I'm sure I'll be fine, thank you.'

'Nonsense,' Liz said quickly. 'You'll stay with me.'

'Thank you,' Jacqueline said. 'I must admit I would feel safer, but what about Will, his place is a mess.'

'Oh, don't worry about me. I'll get the bed sorted out in no time. The rest can wait until tomorrow.'

He did feel a little morose that he wasn't going to get that goodnight kiss though. He certainly felt as if he needed one.

Jacqueline, unbeknown to him, was feeling exactly the same way. They'd had a very pleasant evening, but she'd had an awful start to her day and he'd had a horrible end to his, and nothing would have been nicer than melting into his arms and feeling his lips against hers. There was always tomorrow, but then she shivered. What if John came back and tried to hurt either of them. She wouldn't put anything past him now. She was relieved to hear Sam speak up.

'I think it's safer if you bunk with us tonight, Will. John's obviously in a rotten mood and I think you might sleep better away from your boat.'

Will was about to refuse when Jacqueline spoke.

'Oh what a good idea. I certainly would feel better if you weren't on your own boat tonight.'

'Alright, if you think it's best. Thanks, Sam.'

Will's heart skipped a beat. Jacqueline did care for him and he wondered if he would sleep at all now thinking about her. However, he had more or less forgotten about John and he certainly wouldn't be worrying about him. All his thoughts and dreams would be about Jacqueline tonight.

16

The following day Jacqueline woke up earlier than usual, but Liz had already been up and about for a while.

'Good morning,' Liz said. 'How are you? I couldn't sleep very well at all. After yesterday evening, there was too much going through my mind.'

'I slept solidly for a couple of hours,' Jacqueline replied. 'Then I just kept waking up and when I did drop off again, I had some strange dreams. Will and John were in them, and then Jonathon was there as well, but I can't really remember them now. Oh dear, I do hope the police find John today. I don't feel safe knowing he's out there and wants to hurt Will.'

'And you perhaps.'

'I don't know if he does want to do anything to me. Perhaps he does, but he professes to have feelings for me and resents Will for taking me from him. Well, that's what he thinks anyway. And after all, he did ransack Will's boat and left mine alone. I reckon he thinks that with Will out of the way, he can have me all to himself. That is, until he decides he's in love with Kate again. To think I thought he was a nice guy when I first met him.'

'Appearances can be deceptive,' Liz said. 'Mind you, if it makes you feel any better, I thought he was a very pleasant man for a long time, and in fact we did become pretty good friends. I'm finding it hard to accept this change in him.'

Liz paused for a moment looking sad and Jacqueline didn't really know what to say to her. However, Liz quickly pulled herself back together.

'Anyway, do you fancy a bit of breakfast? I'm quite peckish,' she said.

'I'd love some. I don't think I'll go to the café for breakfast today seeing as Will suggested lunch there. He wants to tidy up his boat this morning and check that nothing's been stolen. I do hope everything's still there,' Jacqueline said, and then shivered. 'Do you think John went to his house last night?'

'I doubt it. I imagine he would have been too clever to go home, and if he's not there, he could be anywhere.'

'If they do find him, I wonder if he'll go to jail for what he's done?' Jacqueline asked.

'Probably not, unfortunately,' Liz replied. 'I expect he'll just get a fine and a slap on the wrist. However, hopefully Daniel will throw him out of the marina.'

'Daniel throw out money! I doubt it!' Jacqueline exclaimed.

'True, but he's got a waiting list of people wanting to get a berth here, so he won't be any worse off.'

'But then Daniel won't have anyone to offload Kate onto, will he?' Jacqueline remarked.

Liz smiled and went to prepare their breakfasts.

* * *

A couple of hours later Jacqueline went into the bar with Will, feeling a little more relaxed. Life wasn't so bad. She was lucky to be with such a wonderful man, the police were looking for John and everybody at the marina was keeping an eye out for him. Would John really have the nerve to come back?

Will and Jacqueline sat down and looked at a menu. Suddenly, he reached over and kissed her. She smiled and kissed him back.

'I missed our goodnight kiss last night,' he said.

'Me too,' she replied, 'But I'm sure we'll have time for plenty more.'

Will grinned, asked her what she wanted for lunch and went to order. He was looking forward to a relaxed meal for two. However, little did he know that they weren't destined to have a quiet romantic meal.

Kate was sitting with her brother, Tony, and his wife, Lucy, on the other side of the café. She kept looking at Will and Jacqueline and they soon noticed that she was staring at them. All of a sudden she stood up.

'I blame you two,' Kate said, looking at Jacqueline and Will. 'John's disappeared because you reported him to the police. As if he'd destroy your boat, Will. He's much too nice to do anything like that. And as for you making up a lie like that,' Kate continued, glaring at Jacqueline. 'Imagining that John fancies you. Huh! He's in love with me. How could you lie to the police like that?'

By this time, Kate's voice had risen and tears had begun to fall. Both Will and Jacqueline were dumbfounded by her public display of emotion, especially as it was directed towards John.

'Be quiet, Kate,' Tony hissed. 'You're making a spectacle of yourself again.'

He tried to pull her back into her seat, but she refused to sit down.

'I'm sorry about this,' Tony said, looking at Will and Jacqueline. 'I just don't know what's got into her.'

'Don't speak about me as if I'm not

here,' Kate screamed. 'They told lies about my John. I hate them.'

'Your John today. Yesterday it was your Daniel. Who will it be tomorrow, Kate?' Tony asked sharply.

'I've had enough of this,' Lucy suddenly spoke.

Her voice was harsh and she startled everybody just by speaking. Lucy rarely said anything.

'Kate, you're embarrassing our family,' Lucy continued.

She grabbed Kate's arm and dragged her out of the bar, surprising everyone with her strength. Tony meekly followed behind, apologising profusely.

'See, I told you,' Jacqueline whispered to Will. 'There is another woman hiding behind that exterior. I wouldn't put it past Lucy having an affair with Arthur.'

Will grinned.

'You do seem to be very interested in the murders don't you, Jacqueline? What about Kate?'

'Oh, I suppose she could have been

having an affair with Arthur!'

'I don't mean that, I mean her behaviour.'

'Well, it was a bit of a shock, but she is very volatile, and if Daniel has been inattentive she's probably turned her attentions back to John. She does like to be the centre of attention as well. She probably enjoys having two men interested in her and can't stand the thought of John being keen on me as well.'

'Are you two okay?' Jim called out. 'I was that close to banning that woman, but it's a bit difficult with Tony being the commodore. Still . . . '

'You'd be well within your rights,' Will remarked. 'We're all used to her, but she'd put off strangers. If Daniel heard about this he wouldn't be too happy. There could have been people in here wanting to moor their boats in the marina. They would be a bit put off by Kate.'

'You're not kidding! I think if I have another display like that in here, I will ban her. To hell with the consequences.'

'I very much doubt that Tony will blame you,' Jacqueline added. 'I heard him having a go at her the other day on his boat. I think he's pretty well fed up with her behaviour. And as for Daniel, I think he might be relieved.'

Cassie came out of the kitchen to join in the conversation.

'Tony often tells Kate off in here as well. By the way, I was sorry to hear about the problems you've both had with John. It's terrible what he did to your boat, Will.'

'If he did do it. It's not been proven yet, but we're pretty sure it was him.'

'Yes, particularly after all the threats he made to me yesterday morning,' Jacqueline added.

Will looked at Jacqueline, thinking how brave she was. He was still in shock, not ever having had anyone hate him with such a vengeance before. He wished the police would find John and he would confess. Will had come to the conclusion that he wouldn't sleep soundly again until John was in police custody. Perhaps John had some psychological problems. He certainly didn't act like a normal person. Kate didn't either, but she seemed more childish than anything else.

Jacqueline could see that Will was deep in thought and she was worried about him. He was more sensitive than she had given him credit for.

'Are you alright, Will?' she asked

'Yes, I think it's all just sinking in how dangerous John is. If he had a motive, I would certainly think he was capable of murder.'

'Do you think so? I don't know. He seemed so nice at first, but he does have a temper. You don't think he might do something to one of us?'

'It has crossed my mind.'

'Will, let's try and think about something else.'

'Okay, but I keep remembering last night.'

'I don't blame you,' Liz said, appearing in the bar. 'Hope you don't mind me disturbing you. Just wanted to grab a quick lunch while it's quiet in the chandlery.'

'No, of course not,' Jacqueline said, although Will's face fell.

'I'll only be ten minutes or so,' Liz said as if she could sense his disappointment.

'Here's your sandwich and a glass of wine,' Cassie said, putting them on the table.

Liz had rung up and ordered ahead.

'Are you two worried that John might try something else,' Liz asked, taking a bite of her sandwich.

'A bit,' Jacqueline replied. 'Will thinks he's capable of murder. I didn't think so when he first mentioned it, but perhaps he's right. He does seem to have a dark side. He could come back in the middle of the night and do anything to either of us. I just wish the police would find him.'

'So do I,' Liz said. 'It's not right that you have to live in fear like this, not right at all.'

Jacqueline and Will then went on to

tell Liz about Kate's outburst and their suspicions of Lucy being Arthur's mistress.

'But alternatively Kate could have been his mistress, don't you think?' Liz said.

Will and Jacqueline both nodded. Anything seemed possible.

'Kate comes across as too flirtatious at times and childish at others, but I think it's a cover for a ruthless personality,' Liz continued. 'She only goes to John when Daniel doesn't want her. Daniel is the richer of the two men and Arthur is even wealthier. He could have showered her with gifts and she'd have been quite happy. It probably wouldn't have mattered that he was so much older and not particularly good looking. Meanwhile, she could still have continued her odd relationships with Daniel and John. Then perhaps Arthur tired of her and ended the relationship, so she poisoned him.'

'Where would she get the poison from at such short notice?' Will asked.

'Perhaps Arthur arranged to meet her and she suspected that he was going to break up with her so she took some poison in case he did. We don't know her past at all. Perhaps she's been involved in such antics before,' continued Liz.

'I still think Lucy is a more likely suspect. You should have seen how firm and strong she was with Kate, Liz,' Jacqueline said. 'Or perhaps it was Penelope after all, but I still think she's the least likely candidate.'

'I agree. I still can't imagine her killing anyone,' Liz said. 'Anyway, I'd better get back to work. By the way, I rang the hospital. There's been no change with Arthur and unfortunately they didn't sound too hopeful. They wouldn't tell me much else though.'

'Poor old Arthur,' Jacqueline said once Liz had gone back to work. 'Perhaps he'll never come out of that coma and he won't be able to tell us who poisoned him.'

'I'm sure that's what the killer is

banking on. It's impossible to get into that hospital room with the police guarding it 24/7, otherwise I'm certain the murderer would have tried to sneak in and finish off the job. Anyway, to change the subject and cheer us up, let's go out this afternoon,' Will said. 'It'll take our minds off all this. There are some lovely gardens to walk round not far from here. They have great tearooms there as well. What do you say?'

'That sounds like a good idea. I'd love to go. I'll just go and change into some more comfortable shoes.'

Will and Jacqueline got up and went out to spend an afternoon away from murders, attempted murders and hysterical women.

17

While Will and Jacqueline were enjoying themselves at Saville Gardens, two police officers stood outside Kate Hunter's house. After her encounter with Will and Jacqueline in the café bar at the Black Swan Marina, she had got straight into her car and driven home. She only lived a couple of miles away in Slough.

The police officers rang the doorbell a couple of times, but there was no answer. As there was a car in the driveway, they started banging at the door thinking there must be someone at home. Finally Kate, imagining that they would never go away, went and answered the door.

'Is there a Mr. John Stevens here?' the police officer asked.

'Who?'

'Mr. John Stevens.'

'I'm afraid I don't know him.'

'We know you do, miss, now please let us in.'

'No, you can't come in,' Kate said, her voice getting higher.

'Let them in,' John said. 'I'm John Stevens. What can I do for you, officers?'

'We have reason to believe that you were involved in an incident at the Black Swan Marina on Tuesday evening.'

'Really, and what might that have been?' John replied, his voice remaining completely calm.

'An incident involving a boat belonging to Mr. William Phillips.'

'I can assure you that I was not involved in any such incident.'

'I will have to ask you to accompany me to the police station to answer a few questions.'

'No,' Kate screamed.

'Shush, dear,' John said, his voice not faltering at all. 'I won't be long. This is just a misunderstanding.'

John kissed Kate on the cheek and

left with the police officers. Kate stood there trembling, with tears flowing down her face.

★   ★   ★

The following day, in the late after-noon, Liz came out of the supermarket in Windsor. She only needed a few things and was glad there weren't too many other shoppers about. Frank wanted to have supper in the bar and she needed to get changed and re-do her make-up before they went in. They were meeting Sam and Pauline at seven so she didn't have a lot of time. As she headed towards the car park, she gasped. There was John walking through town as bold as brass. Liz walked quickly towards him, relieved that she only had a little shopping to carry with her. Reaching him, she put her free hand on his shoulder. John turned around and smiled.

'Liz, how nice to see you.'

Liz was amazed by his attitude.

253

Granted they had been friends for ages, but after what had happened earlier in the week, he had a nerve acting as if he nothing had happened.

'I can't believe you, John, pretending that you've done nothing wrong.'

'Not you as well, Liz?' John replied sadly. 'I thought you were my friend. You know I say things in anger, but I don't really mean them. You don't think I did all that damage to Will's boat, do you?'

'I don't know what to think, John. You've got problems and you don't always take your medication. When you're not on your meds, you can do things you wouldn't dream of doing when you are on them.'

'I promise you, I am taking my meds,' John said. 'I didn't do anything to Will's boat, believe me. Anyway, I've spoken to the police already.'

'You have? So, what did they say?'

'They've taken a statement, but they haven't got enough evidence to prosecute. Come on, Liz, we're friends, have a drink with me.'

'I don't know, John. I feel a little awkward after all that's happened.'

'Just a quick one, please. I don't suppose I'll be welcome at the marina until my name's cleared, so we may not see each other for a while.'

'Alright, I'll give you the benefit of the doubt. After all, we have been friends for a long time.'

★ ★ ★

Later that evening in the bar, Liz told Sam and Pauline about her encounter with John and how he denied tampering with Will's boat. They were sceptical, as was Frank. However, having talked to John, Liz was unsure. However, if John hadn't done it, who had? When Will and Jacqueline joined them later, Liz also told them about meeting John.

'I don't believe him,' Will said. 'I don't believe him one bit.'

'I don't think I do either,' agreed

Jacqueline. 'And are you sure he really has been interviewed by the police?'

'Oh dear,' Liz exclaimed. 'I didn't even think of that. I just believed him. I'm so sorry. He seemed like the old John again. It didn't cross my mind that he could be lying.'

'Don't worry about it,' Jacqueline said. 'I'm sure he thought you would have called the police as soon as you left him. There wouldn't really have been any point in him lying.'

'Do you think we should call them now?'

However, before they could do anything, the door opened and a loud voice filled the room.

'Well, I hope you're all satisfied,' Kate said loudly. 'The police arrested my John yesterday afternoon.'

Liz breathed a sigh of relief.

'And what are you smiling at?' Kate said, staring at Liz.

'I saw John in town this evening, so the police haven't put him in prison.'

'I don't believe you,' Kate replied, the tears starting to flow. 'Why hasn't he come to see me? I can't believe it.'

'Now, now,' Liz said. 'He probably had a difficult time and needs a bit of space. Leave him alone for a bit and go and see him tomorrow. Have a couple of drinks with us and relax. You look really tense. It's not doing you any good and it certainly won't help John.'

Kate was pleasantly surprised by Liz's words and was actually pleased to be invited to join their group. She didn't have that many friends as most of her energies were directed at ensnaring a man, but at this moment she felt as if she needed friends. The situation was getting very stressful and she couldn't find a way to relax. Perhaps she might be able to calm down a little, as long as everybody was nice to her. It didn't cross her mind that she didn't deserve anybody being pleasant to her, but in fact the other people were just hoping she would be quiet! Then Janet entered the room and any hope of a peaceful evening disappeared.

'Pint please,' she shouted to Jim. 'How's everybody?'

They all quickly said they were fine before Kate could say anything about John.

'I hear Arthur's still in a coma,' Janet said.

'I wish they'd let us go and see him.' Liz remarked. 'I'm sure it would do him good to hear familiar voices. I've heard things like that can wake people up out of a coma. I'd be willing to go, as I'm sure many of us here would. He could hold the key to who the murderer is.'

'Perhaps you should suggest it to the police again, Liz,' Will said. 'Maybe get a doctor to back you up. It wouldn't do any harm.'

'Yes,' Jacqueline added. 'I don't know why, but I have an awful feeling that the wrong person is going to pay for these deaths and that only Arthur will be able to tell us who the real killer is.'

18

The following morning Kate woke up at ten on her brother's boat. Tony didn't like her staying on it when he wasn't there, but she didn't care. What did he think she was going to do? Have wild orgies? Take the boat out and crash into another boat? She was well and truly fed up of Tony's attitude towards her. In fact, she had only decided to sleep on the boat because she had been well and truly over the limit and she didn't want to risk losing her license. The thought of having to rely on public transport appalled her.

Kate had enjoyed the previous evening, but now she had a splitting headache. She had drunk too much and she blamed Janet for her fragile condition. That woman really knew how to drink and Kate hadn't wanted to be outdone. However, now she felt as if she'd acted childishly. In fact, she'd been acting stupidly a lot lately, turning her affections from John to Daniel and back to John again. She wished she could be like Jacqueline who was so sophisticated and refined. Jacqueline still had men chasing after her despite not wearing short skirts and lots of make-up. Perhaps she should change her look, but when she had taken some aspirin and had drunk two strong black cups of coffee, Kate couldn't help but put on a thick layer of foundation, thick eyeliner and red lipstick. As she looked at the final result in the mirror, she felt better. This was her style and there was nothing wrong with it. She thought she looked irresistible and decided to go and see if John was all right. She hoped he wasn't upset that she hadn't come to see him since the police had picked him up, but then he hadn't come to tell her how things had gone with them. Let him stew for a bit longer.

Kate hadn't got a change of clothes, but the little red skirt and white blouse she had worn the previous day were still clean, so she slipped them on. She thought she looked perfect, although she was glad Tony and Lucy weren't there. They wouldn't approve of her going out in that outfit, especially during daylight hours. She then fiddled about in her bag for her mobile and called the office where she worked.

'Hello, Mrs. Jones,' she snivelled into the phone, 'It's Kate. I'm so sorry. I've been up all night with a terrible cold and headache. I only dropped off at about six this morning and I've just woken up. I'm afraid I won't be in today.'

As she closed her call, Kate laughed. That Mrs. Jones was so easy to fool. Little did she know that her boss intended to give her a final warning the next time she came into work. Mrs. Jones was fed up of Kate's attitude to her job. She fully suspected Kate wasn't ill at all and everything she had just said was a pack of lies.

Kate decided to go to her house first

to see if John had gone there to wait for her. It was on the way to his house so it made sense to stop there first anyway. John had been so in love with her that he'd wanted to exchange house keys. She thought it was a bit early in their relationship for that, but still, she had agreed. She quite fancied nosing around John's things when he wasn't there, but she doubted he would do the same in her house, so what was the harm?

Getting into her car, Kate wondered if John might have fallen asleep on her sofa and hadn't woken up. He often just dropped off; mainly due to some of the meds he took. She was still surprised however, that he hadn't phoned her at some point. According to Liz, it had been a long time since the police had released him.

Kate stalled her car a couple of times and then decided to drive slowly, knowing that she was still a bit groggy after last night. Eventually she reached her house and went in. She called out for John, but there was no reply. He wasn't on the sofa and the bed didn't look as if it had been slept on. She picked up John's house key from her bedside drawer and looked at it fondly before putting it in her pocket. In reality she was actually proud that he had given it to her. It made her feel wanted, which was something she rarely felt. Both of her parents had been killed in a car crash when she was eighteen and her brother, Tony, didn't like her much and nor did his wife. She had tried to get Daniel to exchange house keys as well, but he had blatantly refused. Daniel certainly didn't want Kate coming to his home unannounced when he might be entertaining another woman. Although Kate usually pretended not to care about things, she did care more than people guessed, and she knew that Daniel felt she wasn't good enough for his circle of friends. It hurt her terribly and this was why she kept turning back to John. He loved her unconditionally and she did try to love him back, but he was dull and quite boring. Every time she saw Daniel, she felt an irresistible pull towards him. She couldn't help herself, but she had to try to resist him. She kept telling herself over and over that John was a much better man than Daniel.

Within fifteen minutes, Kate was at John's home. It was a lovely house, but it wasn't as big as Daniel's. Daniel had taken her there once and the house was enormous. It had its own pool, sauna and games room. That was the way to live, thought Kate. However, if John became a famous artist, he too could own a similar house, but what were the chances of that happening? Kate didn't think much of John's paintings, not that she would ever tell him of course.

Kate opened the front door and went in.

'John, are you here?' she called out loudly

However, again there was no reply, but Kate still decided to take a look around. Perhaps he was asleep. His meds made him sleep very soundly and it took a lot to wake him up. She wandered around downstairs and then looked in the back garden, but there was no sign of him. She went upstairs, first of all glancing in the spare room as it was the first room after the stairs, but that was empty. Then she went into John's bedroom.

'There you are, John,' she said. 'I've been calling you. Have you been taking sleeping tablets again or overdoing your meds? You should stick to the correct dosage of those anti-psychotics of yours, you know?'

John still didn't stir.

'You can ignore me as much as you want, John Stevens, I'm not going anywhere,' Kate continued.

John still didn't move, so Kate went over and shook him. All of a sudden, she screamed. John's face was contorted as if he had had a seizure. Kate knew that he was dead and she dropped to the ground, shaking.

'Oh my God, what am I going to do

now? The police will think I did this. I know they will,' Kate stammered and paused for a moment. 'No, no they won't. John could have been dead for a while and I have an alibi for last night. I'll have to call the police. It's better than running away, isn't it?'

She started crying. Kate was not one to make decisions easily, but she had to now and it had to be the right one. She sat on the only chair in the room and got out her mobile.

'The right thing to do,' she said after a few minutes of taking deep breaths, 'is to call the police. I have to do the right thing for once in my life. I have to.'

★ ★ ★

Twenty minutes later, Detective Jameson arrived. Kate had calmed down by this time and after showing him the body, he sent her down into John's sitting room. Jameson stayed in the bedroom with the pathologist.

'You shouldn't have touched the

body, you know,' Jameson said when he finally sat down with Kate.

'I didn't know he was dead,' she said defensively. 'I thought he was asleep, so I tried to wake him up. So when do you think he died?'

She was terrified he would say this morning and she wouldn't have an alibi.

'The pathologist says between five and nine last night. And where were you at that time?'

'Me, you can't think I killed him?'

'Please answer the question, Miss Hunter.'

Kate frowned. She knew they'd think she killed John.

'Well, I was at work until 6.30. I do flexitime and hadn't started until 10 that morning. You can ask my boss, Mrs. Jones. She was there and so were some other people. Then I drove to the marina. I work in Staines and there was a lot of traffic so it was well after seven when I got there. I went to see if John was on his boat. I hadn't seen him since he'd been arrested you see, and the boat was the first place he might have been on my route home. He wasn't there, but as I went by the café bar, I saw Jacqueline, Janet, and some others in there, so I went in and stayed there all evening. You can ask any of them.'

'Don't worry, we will. I'm surprised you didn't carry on looking for John.'

'I was going to, but then I ended up having a few too many drinks and I couldn't drive with all that alcohol in my system, could I? So, I stayed on my brother, Tony's, boat. What do you think killed John?'

'We'll find out after the coroner's report.'

Kate was getting annoyed that Jameson was being so cagey. At least she had an alibi and they couldn't accuse her of killing him.

'Couldn't it have been suicide?' she then asked. 'I can't imagine anyone wanting to murder John.'

'We'll have a better idea of that later as well. But why do you think it could have been suicide?'

'John was bi-polar. He was fine when he took his meds, but he could act all weird if he didn't take them.'

'That's very interesting. Nobody's bothered to tell us that before.'

'Really? I don't suppose many people know. Anyway, I don't think I have anything else to tell you. Am I free to go then?'

'After we get a signed statement from you, yes. I must say you don't seem to be that bothered by his death, Miss Hunter.'

'Of course I'm bothered,' Kate said, her voice rising. 'I was in love with him once, but now I'm seeing Daniel Harris, the owner of the Black Swan Marina. Can I go now? I really am upset.'

Kate just wanted to go home and lie down. She was tired and miserable. Although she had said she was going out with Daniel, their relationship wasn't at all steady and she had been trying to convince herself to settle down with John. Why did Daniel treat her so well in private, but was ashamed of taking her out with his friends? Now John was dead and any plans to be with him were over. What a bombshell. She'd have to turn her sights back to Daniel. Perhaps she had better change her appearance a little for him. She didn't much want to, but if he wanted a sophisticated woman, he'd get one.

19

'Come in,' Jacqueline said, expecting her next client.

Instead, Detective Jameson walked in. Her heart sank, knowing that he had probably come to tell her that something awful had happened. Perhaps Arthur had died and there would be no chance of him telling them who his mistress was, or maybe someone else had been murdered. It didn't bear thinking about, but for a couple of days she had felt that there was worse to come.

Detective Jameson could see that Jacqueline was expecting more bad news and he hated to be the one to give it to her, but it was his job. At least she had fallen out with John and hopefully wouldn't be too upset.

'Detective Jameson, good afternoon,' she said, looking worried, despite trying to hide her fears. 'How nice to see you, although I expect you're not here on a social call.'

'Unfortunately not, Mrs. Lawrence. I'm afraid I do have some more bad news. Kate Hunter went to the home of John Stevens this morning and found him dead.'

'Oh no, this can't be true,' Jacqueline whispered, tears starting to fall. 'I know things haven't been good between us recently, but we had been friends. However, he was very unpleasant to me this week and he did threaten Will as you know, but I didn't want to see him dead, I really didn't.'

'I'm sure you didn't, Mrs. Lawrence, despite his erratic behaviour. You know he was bi-polar, don't you? It explains a lot,' the detective continued.

'I didn't know that,' Jacqueline replied, sounding genuinely surprised. 'Perhaps he wasn't taking his medication properly and that's why his moods were so up and down all the time. I had a bi-polar friend who messed around with her meds and she was all over the place. Oh dear, this is so awful. You think you could have done something to help but you probably couldn't. It's such a shame. Sometimes John could be nice, but at others, he was a horrible person. But what happened to him? How was he killed?'

'The autopsy points to belladonna again.'

'Belladonna!' Jacqueline exclaimed. 'It sounds like his death is connected to the others then, but why? He didn't seem to have any ties to the Forbes, did he?'

'No,' the detective continued. 'There seems no connection at all. Of course, we could separate the incidents into two pairs, the two shootings and the two poisonings. Penelope and Richard are the most likely suspects in the murders of Donald and Kevin. Then the mistress is the most likely person to have poisoned Arthur. As for John, perhaps he knew something about the mistress and Arthur.'

Jameson stopped talking; realising that he shouldn't be discussing the case with a member of the public, but Jacqueline was so easy to talk to. Still, he'd better stop before he got himself into trouble. He looked at Jacqueline. She was in a world of her own now.

'You're very quiet,' he said

'Yes,' Jacqueline replied. 'I feel there's a missing piece in this jigsaw, but I can't think what it is. I don't know why, but I think Penelope is innocent. She seems to be a very unhappy woman and I can't see her killing anyone. As for Richard, I don't know him at all. If you could find the mistress, perhaps things might be clearer.'

'Yes, it would help a great deal. It's likely to be someone at the marina, but whoever it is has covered their tracks very well. If only Arthur would wake up, the mystery would be solved,' Jameson said, realising he was talking about the case again.

He thought it would be better if he left.

'Anyway, I'll let you get on. I hope you'll be alright. I know this has been a shock for you.'

'Thank you for letting me know about John. It has been upsetting, but you've been very kind.'

Jacqueline sat back in her chair. She wished she could go back to the barge, but she still had one client. She imagined Will holding and comforting her and then kissing her, gently at first and then the passion increasing, his lips desperate for hers. She would forget all about the murders, especially John's, and then she would lead Will into her bedroom. She closed her eyes as she imagined their night of passion.

'Mrs. Lawrence, am I early . . . '

'Oh, Jean, sorry, do come in, you're right on time.'

Jacqueline was disappointed that she had to put her dreams to one side, but she would soon be home. However, as she started to prepare for the session with her client, an image of John flashed before her and she shivered.

A couple of hours later, Jacqueline was back on her barge, hoping that Will would return soon. She didn't want to be alone this evening, but she knew Will had gone to Birmingham and might not be back till late. Impatiently, she decided to phone him.

'Will, hi, what time do you think you'll be back?'

'I'm afraid it won't be until about ten. Are you missing me?' he replied, with a little laugh.'

Jacqueline burst into tears.

'Hey, what's wrong, darling. I haven't upset you, have I?'

'No, of course not,' she said, trying to stop the tears. 'It's John, he was murdered.'

'What? I can't believe it.'

'It's true. And what's more, it looks like it was by the same person who tried to kill Arthur. They found belladonna in his system.'

'But why? What connection did he

have to Arthur? Oh Jacqueline, this is getting crazy. Poor old John. I can't say I liked the guy, especially after what we think he did to my boat, but I didn't want him dead.'

'Me neither. And what's more Detective Jameson said he was bi-polar. He probably didn't take his meds and that's why he acted so strangely. He just needed help and nobody gave it to him.'

'Calm down, we didn't know he was sick, so it's not our fault. Look, I'll be with you as soon as I can, but I have to see another client first. Why don't you go and spend the evening with Liz until I get back? She always cheers you up?'

'Yes, I think I will. If I'm not on the barge when you get home, I'll be on her boat,' Jacqueline said. 'Can't wait to see you.'

'Me neither,' Will replied, imagining holding her in his arms all night.

20

Arthur Forbes' eyes flickered and started to open, but then they closed again. However, there was nobody in the room to see the first signs of Arthur regaining consciousness. Out in the corridor, a policeman stood watch as usual. He wondered why someone had to be on guard twenty-four hours a day. As far as he knew, nobody had tried to break in, although there had been a strange incident the other day when he had accompanied a woman into the room. She had asked a lot of questions about the life support machine and about Arthur's chances of recovering. He had kept an eye on her, but she hadn't tried anything. Mind you, she might have done the man a favour. He could be in that coma forever, and what sort of a life would that be? That was about the only interesting event in the past few days. Apart from that, this job was absolutely boring and he wished the person who had tried to kill Arthur would be caught so he could go back to his normal routine. However, he had no choice but remain where he was. He had been ordered to stop anyone from killing Arthur Forbes, and that was what he was going to do.

★　★　★

Back at the marina, Jacqueline sat on her barge thinking. She was sure that everything revolved around Arthur and she was almost certain there was just one killer and that was the mistress, but she had no idea why she had also killed Donald, Kevin and John. If only Arthur would wake up. Then the mystery might be solved.

Finally Jacqueline decided she couldn't sit alone on her barge until Will arrived home. He was right; she should go over to Liz's. She hoped Liz wouldn't mind if she just turned up. However, they were good friends, so she probably wouldn't. Jacqueline went to her fridge and got out a bottle of wine to take over.

A few minutes later, Jacqueline knocked at Liz's door.

'Hello,' Liz said.

'Hi, I hope you don't mind me coming over. Will won't be home till late and after hearing about John, I don't feel like being alone.'

'Of course not, come in, I'm just about to make dinner, so why don't you join me. It's been an awful day, hasn't it?'

'Yes, very much so. And I'd love to stay for dinner. Here, I've brought some wine.'

'Great, let's have a glass straight away. I think we need it.'

Jacqueline went on board and sat down, feeling a little more relaxed at last. Liz opened the wine and they both took a large gulp.

'I can't believe that John's gone,' Liz said. 'We were friends for a long while, until Kate came along really. I tried to get him to end his relationship with her. It was very destructive, but he wouldn't have it. He was head over heels in love with her. It eventually built up a barrier between us.'

'I can imagine. Oh, by the way, I expect you know, but Detective Jameson said he was bi-polar.'

'Yes, I did know,' Liz replied. 'He didn't manage his meds well either. He was so nice when he took them properly. It really is sad. He was such a wonderful artist as well. He could have been famous if he had more confidence in himself.'

'I feel so guilty,' Jacqueline said, tears welling up.

'Why?' Liz asked. 'You have nothing to feel guilty about.'

'I wasn't nice to him in the end.'

'He didn't deserve you to be nice to him. Anyway, you didn't know he was going to die. Come on, stop crying. It's not your fault,' she said, putting an arm round Jacqueline. 'That's enough talk about John. Let's try and relax. We need to keep our minds off the murders and have as pleasant an evening as we can.'

They both sipped their wine, not saying much. Jacqueline started to calm down and soon stopped crying. Liz decided it was time to prepare dinner.

'It's just Spaghetti Bolognese. Is that alright?'

'That's great,' Jacqueline said, finishing her second glass of wine. 'I'd better slow down on the wine though before I fall down.'

'I think we both need a few drinks tonight. Might cheer us up a bit. Must pop to the loo first. There's another bottle of red in that cupboard down there,' Liz said, pointing. 'Can you get it out and open it up.'

'Sure,' Jacqueline replied, deciding that Liz was right. A few glasses of wine would be justified tonight.

Jacqueline opened the cupboard door and took out the bottle, but as she moved it, a packet fell onto the floor. When she picked it up, she noticed it was a packet of homeopathic medicine.

Jacqueline gasped when she saw the word belladonna written on it. For a moment, she was unable to move, but then she quickly put the packet back and shut the cupboard door before Liz returned. She was shaking, but she had to open the wine otherwise Liz would know something was wrong. It must have just been a coincidence she thought to herself. Belladonna from a homeopathic surgery wouldn't be that strong. Liz would have had to put a lot of it into a drink to attempt to kill somebody and they might have noticed the taste. But perhaps she had got that packet for herself at some time and that's what had given her the idea. Perhaps somehow she had managed to get hold of stronger belladonna. But no, Liz couldn't be the killer. Liz was her friend and she was in love with her husband. She would never have an affair. Suddenly Jacqueline heard the toilet flush and she hurried to get the corkscrew.

'Ah good, you've found it,' Liz said.

Liz started cooking while Jacqueline tried hard to think of things to say.

'This is nice wine,' she said a little later, unable to find anything else to talk about.

'It is,' Liz replied. 'Pour a bit in the Bolognese sauce and then top up our glasses.'

'Will do,' Jacqueline said, trying to sound normal.

Jacqueline took a large gulp of wine.

'Dinner's almost ready,' Liz said not a moment too soon for Jacqueline. 'Get the knives and forks out please.'

Jacqueline did as she was told. She was scared. The more she thought about it, the more she believed it wasn't a coincidence. Liz was the killer and she was having dinner with her. How could she keep her cool until Will got home? She had become very quiet and she desperately tried to think of something else to say, but couldn't.

'Are you alright?' Liz asked. 'You've gone very quiet.'

'Sorry, I keep thinking about John. I

must try and put him out of my mind.'

'Yes, you must. You've got nothing to feel guilty about.'

Jacqueline tried to smile as she took another sip of wine. Her head was spinning and she knew she'd had too much to drink too quickly. She wished she'd stayed at home and not seen the belladonna. Liz thought that Jacqueline had become very strange since she had gone to the toilet and couldn't imagine why. Then it dawned on her. She kept her belladonna in the cupboard where the bottle of wine had been. It wasn't the belladonna she had used as a poison, but the one she had for her irritable bowel syndrome. However, that wouldn't have made any difference to Jacqueline. She would have seen the word belladonna and that would have been it. She would have known that Liz Boyle was the killer. She hadn't wanted this to happen. She really did like Jacqueline. They had become good friends very quickly and she didn't want to kill her.

However, now she had no choice.

'You know, don't you?' Liz asked Jacqueline.

'Know what?' Jacqueline replied quietly. She had started shaking.

'That I'm the killer.'

'The thought never crossed my mind, Liz. I think I'd better go home. I don't feel very well,' Jacqueline said.

She got up, but stumbled, having had too much to drink.

'I don't think so,' Liz said, grabbing an ornament close to her.

She lunged at Jacqueline and hit her over the head. Jacqueline saw the ornament coming towards her, but before she could even think of moving, it hit her and she fell. Everything went black, and to Liz's delight Jacqueline passed out. Liz got some thick rope, thinking how handy it was that rope was usually kept on boats, and tied both Jacqueline's hands and feet together. She laid her down on the settee, untied the ropes of the boat, started the engine and left the marina.

* * *

Half an hour later, Jacqueline woke up with a splitting headache. She tried to move, but her hands were tied behind her back and she saw her feet were tied up as well. She remembered what had happened and a couple of tears fell. She couldn't believe that her friend, Liz, could have done this to her. What was going to happen now? She had discovered that Liz was the killer and she was certain that she was going to die as well.

Where was Liz? Jacqueline realised that the boat was moving and wondered where Liz was taking her? The thought then occurred that Liz was going to throw her overboard and she would end up dead in the river like Donald. Was Liz going to shoot her first or was she going to leave her tied up and throw her in? Jacqueline had a vision of Liz laughing while watching her sink and drown. That would be worse than being shot first.

No, Jacqueline wouldn't let her do it. She'd have to think of a way of escaping. But how? She'd have to stall her. She'd ask her how she'd committed all the murders. Killers liked to brag. Liz had had to keep it all in, but she'd killed three people and put one in a coma. Detective Jameson thought there were two killers, but Jacqueline was certain that Liz had committed all three murders and had tried to kill Arthur.

Jacqueline tried to loosen the ropes around her wrists, but Liz had tied them too firmly. She started to cry, thinking that it couldn't end like this, not when she'd just started a new life and had met Will. She was falling in love with him and she had never thought she could love again after Jonathon. Then she heard the boat slow down. What was happening? Liz must be going to tie the boat up. Was this it? Was Liz going to kill her now?

A few minutes later, Liz came below deck.

'You're awake then?' was all she said.

'You don't have to do this,' Jacqueline said, stammering. 'We're friends.'

'I don't want to, believe me, but I have no choice.'

'Yes you do. Just give yourself up. You'll get caught eventually. One less death will be better for you.'

'Who says I'll get caught? I have no intention of that happening.'

Jacqueline thought this was the time to get her talking.

'Detective Jameson thinks there were two killers, but there weren't, were there? You did it all, didn't you?'

Liz smiled as all thoughts of getting rid of Jacqueline immediately faded. She had waited a long time to boast about her achievements and finally she could tell somebody how clever she had been.

'Of course. I was amazing, truly amazing. However, I didn't plan to kill anyone originally. It was going to be so simple. Arthur was going to divorce Penelope and marry me. That is, after I divorced Frank of course.'

'I thought you loved Frank, you seemed so happy together.'

'I did, I still do, but he couldn't give me the things I wanted. Arthur could.'

'So you love him as well.'

'I wouldn't go that far.'

'But how could you? I mean . . . '

'What, sleep with him? Ha, it's amazing what money can make you do!'

Jacqueline looked at Liz as if she were seeing a new person. This wasn't the woman she had become friends with. She felt a tear fall and wished she were able to wipe it away before Liz saw it, but the other woman was too engrossed in her story to notice.

'However, time went on and Arthur kept stalling about the divorce, saying that Penelope would want too much in the settlement. That's when I got the idea about Donald. What if he were dead? He wasn't married. The other brother, Richard had been disowned. Arthur would get everything, the business, Donald's house, his money, and believe me, he wasn't short of a bob or two. So I had to keep an eye out for an opportunity. However, in the meantime that Kevin in the chandlery found out about Arthur and me. He saw us kissing and he blackmailed Arthur. He said he would tell Penelope if Arthur didn't give him a thousand pounds every month. That was ridiculous. He was a slimy little thief. Then he asked me for five hundred a month. I wasn't going to have that, so he had to go as well. That fateful week, everything came together. Arthur told me Donald was coming to the boat for a few days. I had to work out a plan, a clever plan. I wouldn't have a chance like this again for a long time. Well, I found out that Donald was coming down on Wednesday afternoon on the train. Arthur and I both came to the marina on Tuesday without our other halves. Arthur made excuses to Penelope and me to Frank so we could spend time alone. Arthur and I spent the night and the following day together. Quite late on Tuesday night, I made an excuse that I had to get something from my boat, but I took Arthur's car keys as well. We'd just made love and he was dozing as usual, so he didn't know how long I was away. I went to the car park. Nobody was about, so I opened the bonnet of Arthur's car, removed the fuse from the engine fan and sealed the fuse box with super glue. It took no time at all. When I got back to the boat, Arthur was fast asleep. The following day, I made sure he didn't use his car until he had to go and pick up his brother.'

'And then what?' Jacqueline asked. 'You really did have it all planned down to the last detail, but how on earth did you kill Donald? You're quite a small woman and he was a large man.'

'You don't need to be that big if you've got a gun,' Liz said and then laughed. 'Well, the next thing I did was go to the station. I made up a sign with Donald's name on it and stood waiting for the train, holding the sign like they do at the airport.'

Jacqueline nodded, thinking that Liz had nerves of steel. After all, Arthur's car could have got him to the station before the engine overheated.

'Anyway,' Liz continued. 'Donald got off the train and I met him. I told him that Arthur had twisted his ankle and had sent me to pick him up. He wasn't suspicious at all and got into my car without asking any questions.'

'And Arthur's engine did overheat as you hoped?'

'Yes it did and as Donald doesn't have a mobile so Arthur couldn't contact him. Fancy not having a mobile in this day and age, but Donald hates them, and it certainly did me a favour.'

'So what did you do once you drove away from the station? It can't have been easy to kill him.'

'On the contrary,' Liz replied. 'It was as easy as pie. Well, I was a bit nervous. It was my first time as a killer after all. I drove for a little while and then I pretended I had to pop to my boat. I said it was moored just like yours used to be, on the bank of the river. I drove down a quiet road I knew. Donald was none the wiser. Then I pretended to feel sick. I stopped the car and apologised and said I was just getting out for a bit of fresh air. I got out of the car and went round to Donald's door, opened it and pointed my gun at him. You should have seen his face. He was shocked. Couldn't understand what I was doing or why. 'Get out,' I said. My voice was completely steady and calm. He did as I said. I think he thought he could talk me out of killing him, but my mind was set. He asked me why I was doing this, but I told him to shut up. I ordered him to walk towards the river and when he reached the edge, he stopped. I told him to turn and he did. He looked terrified. Then I told him about me and Arthur and why he had to die. He begged me not to kill him. He told me he'd give me lots of money, but of course, it wouldn't work out like that. He'd tell the police and I'd go to jail.

Arthur would end our relationship and would stay with Penelope. It was too late. I had no choice but to carry it through. Donald had to die. I looked at him and apologised. Then I shot him and he fell back into the river. It was deep there and he started sinking straight away. God, how ironic that he should surface at the marina! I looked around, but luckily there was nobody to be seen. I went back to my car and drove home to Frank. It's funny that Arthur didn't suspect that I had killed Donald, but he didn't. I suppose it all seemed a bit farfetched really. I had kept talking about Richard that day as well and perhaps I planted the idea of his younger brother being the killer. I imagine Arthur couldn't work out why I would kill Donald before he had left Penelope. Quite a clever move don't you think?'

'What about Kevin then?' Jacqueline asked, wanting to stretch the conversation out for as long as possible. However, she had no idea what good that would do. They were way out on the river in the dark. Would anybody find them before Liz killed her?

'Ah, Kevin, the blackmailer. Arthur told me that Kevin was blackmailing him, but I didn't tell him that Kevin had started to blackmail me. I thought it would be less likely that he would suspect me to be the killer if he didn't know. On that Friday evening, Frank and I arrived at the marina at about eight in the evening. I noticed Kevin was still in the chandlery when we arrived. We'd brought a takeaway and after we'd had that, Frank went to have a shower. Meanwhile, I went to the chandlery and shot Kevin. Frank was still in the shower when I got back. The chandlery wasn't open. Kevin was doing his books, so I had no fear of being disturbed. It really was easy.'

'They do say murder gets easier after the first one,' Jacqueline commented.

'They do, but it wasn't so easy with Arthur. I suppose I do love him in a strange way. Not in the way I love

Frank. I suppose it surprises you that I would leave Frank for him, but although I love Frank, life is a little dull. Arthur buys me beautiful gifts and we did plan to travel all over the world.'

'Didn't Frank notice you were having an affair?'

'No, not Frank. He's not the most observant man on earth and he certainly can't tell the difference between expensive and cheap clothes or jewellery, so I got away with a lot. And Arthur listened to me, he really did. Frank likes his football you see.'

'Penelope wouldn't agree that Arthur listens.'

'Ha, not to her. He fell out of love with her many years ago. Arthur was in love with me.'

'Yet you tried to kill him?'

'He decided that Penelope was going to take too much in the divorce settlement. That's why he called it off. He's like me. He needs the best things in life. We both don't want to live in poverty. But I'd killed Donald for him.

We'd have had his money. I had killed two men for him and I wasn't going to let him live.'

Jacqueline was starting to become scared again and didn't think she could reason with Liz.

'So why the belladonna?' Jacqueline asked. 'Mind you, I wouldn't have thought that the homeopathic stuff would be strong enough.'

'It's not. I got that for my irritable bowel syndrome, but it didn't work too well. However, I met someone in the homeopath's waiting room who offered to get me some stronger belladonna. They told me to be careful with it, as it could be dangerous. That's what I put in Arthur's coffee. He didn't even see me do it. I was certain he was almost dead when I left him, but I should have waited to make sure. Now there's no way to get into his hospital room to disconnect his life support machine. I just hope he never wakes up.'

Jacqueline cringed. Liz was a hard and evil woman. She knew now that Liz wouldn't hesitate to kill her. She had to stall her a little longer. Then she remembered the letter from Penelope to Kevin.

'Did Penelope really write that letter to Kevin? Were they really having an affair?' Jacqueline asked.

'Of course not,' Liz laughed. 'It was clever though, wasn't it? It gave the police something else to think about.'

'And what about John? What did he have to do with anything?' Jacqueline asked.

'Nothing. I did that for you.'

'What?' Jacqueline exclaimed. 'Oh my God, I feel sick. Why, why for me?'

'Because you're my friend and he was frightening you and Will. It had to stop. I bumped into him in Windsor and he invited me for a drink, but then he said he had finished the painting he was doing for me, so I went to his house to collect it. While I was there, we had a drink and I managed to slip in the belladonna. It wasn't difficult at all.'

Jacqueline couldn't believe what she

was hearing. She looked at Liz. Her face was immovable and still. Was this what a truly mad person looked like?

'Now, what to do with you,' Liz said.

'Please, please, don't hurt me,' Jacqueline begged.

'Believe me, I don't want to,' Liz replied. 'But I have no choice, no choice whatsoever. It's my own fault. If only I hadn't asked you to get the wine. Then you'd have been none the wiser and we could have stayed friends.'

'The police would have found out it was you in the end and you would have gone to jail. Then we wouldn't have stayed friends.'

'Really?' Liz said. 'I can't imagine that you wouldn't have come to visit me in prison, I can't imagine that at all.'

Liz smiled, while the tears started to fall down Jacqueline's cheeks.

21

The nurse entered Arthur Forbes' room to check that everything was all right.

'Oh my goodness, Mr. Forbes, you're awake,' she said excitedly.

Arthur's eyes were open and he was looking around. He tried to speak, but nothing came out.

'Don't say anything yet, I'll get the copper.'

A few seconds later, the police officer was in the room. He was shocked. He had never expected the man to ever wake up from his coma.

'I'd better ring the boss,' he said to the nurse. 'He'll want to get over here as soon as possible. Mr. Forbes will probably know who the killer is.'

'Don't tire him out,' the nurse said. 'I'm going to get the doctor.'

★ ★ ★

Half an hour later, Detective Jameson appeared on the scene. The doctor had already examined Arthur.

'It appears that Mr. Forbes is now talking a little,' the doctor said. 'But he needs rest.'

'I understand,' Jameson said. 'I just have one simple question for him and I'll be on my way.'

Detective Jameson went into Arthur's room.

'Good evening Mr. Forbes, nice to have you back with us. Thought you'd never wake up again!'

Arthur attempted a weak smile.

'I just have one question for you. Who tried to kill you? Can you remember?'

'Yes, Arthur stammered. 'Liz, Liz Boyle.'

Detective Jameson was shocked. She seemed such a nice woman. Was she Arthur's mistress? Did she really try and kill him? Did she kill John as well? Perhaps Jacqueline had been right and she had also killed Donald and Kevin.

302

He had better get down to the marina as soon as possible before she tried to kill anyone else.

Jameson got into his car with another police officer and drove to the marina, cursing the traffic all the way. It was only a few miles from Slough to Windsor, but it took him over half an hour. He had a bad feeling, but he didn't know why. It must be Jacqueline's influence. She had kept saying she had a sense of foreboding. Now it was rubbing off on him. When he finally reached the marina, he saw Will in the car park.

'Good evening, Detective Jameson,' Will said. 'Is there a problem? I'm a bit worried myself. I've been trying to call Jacqueline, but she's not been picking up. I've just got back from Birmingham.'

'Arthur's woken up. He said it was Liz who tried to kill him.'

'Oh no,' Will said. 'Jacqueline was having dinner with her. Something must have happened.'

'Calm down, we'll go and see first before panicking. You go and check Jacqueline's boat first.'

Will rushed to the barge, but there was no reply. Then he dashed over to where Liz's boat should have been, but the police officers stood next to an empty space.

'The boat's gone,' Jameson said, stating the obvious.

'So has Jacqueline. Liz has got her. She's going to kill her. I know she is.'

Will was panicking. He couldn't lose Jacqueline now. She was the most amazing woman he had ever met and they had only just started to get to know each other. He would never forgive himself if Liz killed her. He had told Jacqueline to go and spend the evening with a murderer. It would be his fault if she died.

'Now, sir, calm down, it may not be too late. How quick is your boat?'

'It can do about 18 knots, but you're not allowed to do that on the river.'

'I think we can break a few rules if

someone's life is at risk, don't you?'

'I suppose so, but which way will they have gone?'

'I have no idea,' Jameson replied, 'but let's stop talking and get going.'

The three police officers and Will rushed over to Will's boat and got on board. Will started the engine and the officers helped to untie the ropes.

'I'm not very good at this, sir,' one of them said.

'You're doing great,' Will replied.

He wasn't, but Will didn't want to put him off. Any help was better than none.

'So,' Jameson said. 'What do you reckon? You know more about the river than I do. Which way shall we go?'

'I reckon upstream, it's quieter. If she went downstream, she'd end up in Windsor. It's too busy and she might be seen dumping a body.'

Will shivered, imagining Liz dropping Jacqueline's body in the river. No, it wasn't going to happen. They'd get there in time. He realised at that moment that he'd fallen in love with Jacqueline and it couldn't end now. He only hoped she'd had dinner with Liz first and that they had only just gone out. Liz's boat wasn't fast. He reckoned it only did four or five knots. He also hoped that Liz might hesitate. He knew Liz liked Jacqueline and she wouldn't want to kill her. Perhaps she would delay the inevitable. Jacqueline was clever as well and would try and stall her. Will hoped Jacqueline would ask Liz how she had committed the murders. Most murderers liked to brag, and Liz would be proud of her accomplishments. But why had Liz decided to kill Jacqueline? Jacqueline must have discovered something. That was the only likely explanation.

'You seem deep in thought, sir,' Jameson asked Will.

'Yes, I reckon Jacqueline must have found something out, otherwise Liz would never have tried to hurt her. They were good friends.'

'Hopefully Jacqueline might try and

stall her,' Jameson said.

'I was thinking that. Jacqueline will probably ask how she committed the murders and Liz will go through all the details. That should take some time.'

'Yes, killers are often keen to show off, especially if they have committed murders with elaborate plots,' Jameson said.

Once on the Thames proper, Will sped up. It was late so there shouldn't be any river police about. Anyway, if there were, Jameson would explain the situation and they would no doubt help, but it would take up valuable time. They had to find Liz's boat as soon as possible, but she could have tied up anywhere in the dark. Luckily Will had lots of torches on board which he gave to the officers. They scanned the banks of the river, but Will was the only one who really knew what Liz's boat looked like and he was terrified he would miss it. He felt as if they were looking for a needle in a haystack, but what else could they do? This was their only chance of finding Jacqueline alive. However, before getting to the lock, one of the officers shouted out,

'I can see two women on deck over there.'

'Quiet,' Jameson said. 'Can you slow down, Will?'

'Sure, so you think it's them?'

'It's possible. Can you go over slowly? Don't want to frighten Liz if it is her.'

Will slowed right down and moved the boat over towards the bank. Jameson called out.

'Mrs. Boyle. Is that you? If you have Mrs. Lawrence, let her go and then we can talk.'

There was silence for a moment and then Liz spoke.

'Never. What is there to talk about?'

'Arthur's awake. He said you tried to kill him.'

'Awake! Huh. There's no killing him, is there? But I killed John, Donald and Kevin and soon Jacqueline will be dead as well.'

'No,' Will shouted. 'Please, Liz, there's no need to kill Jacqueline now.'

'Yes there is. If it weren't for her, I wouldn't be in this position. She must pay.'

'No, please, Liz, you two were friends. Jacqueline, are you alright.'

'At the moment, Will,' Jacqueline called out. 'I knew you'd come.'

'I love you,' he said.

'I love you too,' she replied.

'Enough of that,' Liz screamed. 'It'll do you no good. I've made up my mind.'

With that, she pushed Jacqueline overboard and then dashed off her boat. Jacqueline was still tied up, but Will noticed and jumped straight in.

'Hey,' Jameson called. 'What about the boat?'

He watched Will swim after Jacqueline and saw Liz run away. One of his officers came up.

'I've had a bit of experience with boats so I'll have a go, sir.'

'Thanks,' Jameson said, not holding

out much hope.

Will, meanwhile, was dragging Jacqueline out of the water and untying the ropes around her wrists and ankles. Luckily, he had a penknife with him.

'I thought I'd lost you,' he said as his lips touched hers.

'Me too,' she said, coughing a bit and then laughing as she attempted to kiss him back.

They were disturbed by Will's boat banging against the bank.

'Hey, mind my boat.'

'Well, you did desert us,' Jameson said.

'Jacqueline was thrown in the water all tied up,' Will said defiantly.

'I know, 'Jameson replied, smiling. 'Now, to catch that mad woman,' he continued, as he dashed off into the woods followed by the other officers, leaving Will to tie up his boat.

'Poor Frank,' Jacqueline said.

'I know. It's going to come as a terrible shock to him. Whoever would have thought it was Liz? Did she tell you everything?'

'Yes, she's a very intelligent, but evil woman. It's a pity she didn't use her intelligence in a more constructive way.'

Suddenly, Jacqueline became dizzy and almost fainted.

'Are you alright?' Will asked, taking her into his arms.

'Yes, it's just been a traumatic evening.'

Will looked into her eyes and then kissed her again, his lips anxious for hers. She kissed him back, as desperate for him as he was for her. She couldn't believe how much her life had changed in such a short period of time and that she had met someone who had managed to win her heart over. She didn't feel at all guilty and knew that Jonathon would have given her his blessing.

22

The following day Will and Jacqueline walked into the café bar, having spent a wonderful night together on the barge. Jacqueline was glowing, having almost forgotten about her evening with Liz. However, as they entered the bar, she was surprised to hear loud cheers. Janet, who was with Sam and Pauline, had stood up and had started the cheering. Behind the bar, Jim and Cassie were clapping and Jeff, who was sitting at the bar, shouted out 'hurray' a few times.

'What's all this then?' Jacqueline asked, blushing a little.

She was completely bewildered, not thinking that she had done anything to deserve such a welcome.

'We heard how brave you were last night, Jacqueline,' Janet said. 'And if it wasn't for you, Liz would probably still be walking free. She might have gone on to kill somebody else.'

'No, I wasn't at all brave,' Jacqueline replied. 'It really was very frightening. Do you know if the police caught Liz?'

'Yup,' Janet said, grinning. 'She got up to the road, but fell over and twisted her ankle. Jameson had called for backup and they were waiting for her. Hard to believe Liz was the killer, isn't it? I'm sure it shook you up, Jacqueline? You two had become good friends.'

'Yes, it has been very upsetting,' she said, almost in tears.

Will put his arm around Jacqueline. He hated to see her like this and knew it would take her a while to get over the past few weeks, especially the previous evening. He couldn't imagine how she must have felt thinking she was about to die. He would do everything he could to help her get over it.

Daniel then walked into the bar, and seeing Jacqueline, went over to her.

'How are you? Last night must have been awful for you. I'm pleased to see you're up and about.'

'I'm alright,' Jacqueline replied. 'It'll take me a while to put it to the back of my mind.'

'I'm sure it will. But at least, thanks to you, we can all feel safe now. Everybody's next drink on me, Jim,' he shouted.

A tear flowed down Jacqueline's cheek. She remembered John calling him Santa Claus when he had said the same thing a little while ago. Poor John. He hadn't deserved to die.

'Come and sit with us,' Janet said to Will and Jacqueline.

This time Will didn't mind sharing her with their friends. He'd spent the whole night with her and there were many more to come.

As they went to sit down, the door opened and everyone turned to look. They were all stunned, especially Daniel. It was Kate, but she wasn't wearing her usual short skirt and layers of make-up. She still looked trendy, but her skirt was just above the knee and her make-up had been delicately applied to accentuate her green eyes and delicate bone structure. Daniel couldn't stop staring at her. She smiled at everyone at Jacqueline's table, inwardly feeling very smug, knowing that they were all surprised to see her dressed as she was. She walked towards the bar where Daniel was standing.

'Hello, Daniel,' she said.

'Kate, hello,' he replied, stunned. 'You look amazing.'

'Thank you,' she said modestly.

'Can I buy you a drink?' he asked.

'That would be lovely. A white wine please.'

Daniel was surprised. She usually drank lagers or tia marias and coke. She was a completely different woman today and he definitely liked this change in her.

Over at Jacqueline's table, everybody was surprised to see the new Kate.

'I wonder how long this will last,' Janet commented. 'I doubt if she'll manage to remain sophisticated for more than a day or two.'

'Oh come on Janet, give her a chance. Perhaps she's decided to grow up,' Jacqueline said.

Janet shook her head. In her mind, leopards never changed their spots.

They all watched Daniel and Kate take their drinks and sit together at a corner table. Daniel was mesmerised and Will was certain that he had never seen him look at Kate like that before.

'I hope they find love like we have,' Jacqueline whispered in his ear.

'Me too,' Will replied. 'There's nothing to beat it.'

They looked at each other and kissed, not caring that everybody was watching.

★ ★ ★

Liz Boyle was charged with three counts of first degree murder and two of attempted murder, and went to prison for life. Her husband, Frank, couldn't believe that the woman he loved was a cold-blooded killer, nor that she had been having an affair with Arthur Forbes. However he refused to give up on her and visited her in prison, never filing for divorce. He felt too embarrassed to go back to the marina, sold his boat there and nobody saw him again. Penelope was relieved that Arthur was still alive, but she didn't want to go back to the miserable life they had shared. She asked for a divorce and Arthur gave it to her readily, despite knowing he would be on his own. Like Penelope, he also didn't want to live with someone he didn't love anymore. Penelope and Richard continued their romance and eventually married. Kate, shocked by John's death, decided to change and act her age. She started to take her job more seriously and began to dress sensibly. However, she was still very attractive and Daniel liked the new Kate. Before long, he decided it was time to settle down with her. Will and Jacqueline soon got engaged and decided to live on her barge, keeping his boat to take out on the river. Peace finally reigned again at the Black Swan Marina and Jacqueline was relieved to never see a black swan there again!

THE END

We do hope that you have enjoyed reading this large print book.

Did you know that all of our titles are available for purchase?

We publish a wide range of high quality large print books including:
Romances, Mysteries, Classics
General Fiction
Non Fiction and Westerns

Special interest titles available in large print are:
The Little Oxford Dictionary
Music Book, Song Book
Hymn Book, Service Book

Also available from us courtesy of Oxford University Press:
Young Readers' Dictionary
(large print edition)
Young Readers' Thesaurus
(large print edition)

For further information or a free brochure, please contact us at:
Ulverscroft Large Print Books Ltd.,
The Green, Bradgate Road, Anstey,
Leicester, LE7 7FU, England.
Tel: (00 44) 0116 236 4325
Fax: (00 44) 0116 234 0205

VET IN DEMAND

Carol Wood

For Elissa Hart, the shock of her father's sudden death is bad enough. To find his veterinary practice in such a poor state, both financially and with dated equipment, is just as upsetting. The only way to save the practice is to take on a partner able to make a real investment — and Adam Kennedy is willing to do just that. Can Elissa reconcile her resentment of Adam and his bold ideas with her growing attraction to him?

THE SHAPE OF SUMMER

Barbara Cust

When Anna Blakeney is offered the temporary job of looking after the Chatham children, Sara and Jeremy, her guilty feelings about the deaths of their parents in the car which Anna's father was driving make it impossible for her to refuse. She instantly dislikes the children's half-brother and guardian, Drewe, but while he is away she reckons she can sort out her problems with her boyfriend Ricky. Then Ricky meets someone new, and Anna is surprised to find that her own passions have changed in the most unpredictable way . . .

ESCAPE FROM THE PAST

Iris Weigh

Driving northward in the hope of leaving behind her old life and painful memories, Clare Bowers takes a wrong turn in the mist and ends up in a ditch, from which she is rescued and taken to stay at Moorlands Farm. The owners have had their own tragedies in the past, and there is still a bitter feud between them and the Laytons at the nearby farm. Then Clare meets the darkly handsome Richard Layton, and her past threatens to overtake her again . . .